Introduction By: Reverend Joseph Girzone
Author of Joshua

One of the most difficult problems for people to comprehend is: Why does God allow little children to suffer, or to be born medically fragile? While many people have tried to address that problem, no one has ever adequately answered it. I could not count the number of parents, especially mothers, who have told me that their child who was born with serious defects, especially those with Downs's syndrome, turned out to be the greatest blessing of their life. While I was unable to understand what they meant, I was impressed with what they were telling me, especially since I was aware of the tremendous difficulties and anguish they had to face for so many years. God has his ways, and we will never be able to understand why God allows so many people's lives to be struck with devastating hardships.

In reading the manuscript of Born Under A Lucky Star, I was impressed by the simplicity of the story, which even a child could read and enjoy, but also by Anthony Morrone's very sensitive insight into the mind and heart of a child who had been born severely disabled, and how as a child he grappled within himself why he was so afflicted. The story touches on his relationships with a difficult brother who was hurting because his handicapped brother got so much attention. It deals with relationships with parents and grandparent, and with friends, even a "girl friend," and also with imaginary friends. The playful humor in all these relationships reflects the happy spirit of this little boy, whom some might only pity, and wonder why he was allowed to be born. But, the wisdom and insight that permeates this beautiful story, approaches in a very sensitive way, how God brings joy, happiness, and purpose into the life of one whom many without faith will never understand.

Born Under
A Lucky Star

a medically fragile boy,
a starless Christmas Eve Night,
a lesson of hope.

written by
Anthony L. Morrone
Illustrations by: Daniel Pejril

This book is a work of fiction. Names, characters, places, and incidents are the product of the author's imagination or are used fictitiously. Any resemblance to actual events, locales, or persons, living or dead, is coincidental.

Copyright © 1997 by Anthony Morrone
All rights reserved.

Star Publishing Co.
527 Townline Road
Hauppauge, NY 11788
E-mail at luckystarpublishing.com

Published by
Star Publishing Company

Printed in the United States of America
First Printing: December 2002
Printed by: Unique Business Services
10 9 8 7 6 5 4

Preassigned Control Number: pbb45277
Morrone, Anthony L.
Born Under Lucky Star / Anthony L. Morrone

Book design by Freydoon Rassouli
Illustrations by Daniel Pejril

Acknowledgments

To all the special people who have graced my life, especially:

To Uncle Bill for showing me how to laugh,
To the Camera man for painting a picture of happiness and for developing
     the negative without complaint,
To my parents for being my greatest blessing,
To my precious Patricia for loving me for my very existence,
To Bobby for singing a happy tune for all to hear,
To Katelyn for bringing pure joy to my life,
To Jennifer (my Leigh-Lee girl) for being an exquisite beauty in every way,
To Michael for being a caring person,
To Walt for being a best friend,
To Tommy for sharing his good news with me,
To Larry for teaching me to live for today,
To J.M. for sharing his honesty with me,
To Dan for his uncompromising integrity,
To Uncle Frank for his lesson of trust . . . from his casket,
To Joanne for teaching me to be more patient for change,
To Father Larry for his insight which led me to Chapter II of my story,
To Jill and Paul for editing my scattered thoughts,
To Robert for inspiring me to write this book in a roundabout way,
To K for being a big man with a bigger heart,
To the STAR in my life for shining on me every moment of every day, a
    true friend, whom I lean on constantly for support.
To the gift of being *born under a lucky star*, in good times and in bad.

     And to all of you who dream that a wish on a STAR can come true. It can happen with a little hope and a simple prayer; the impossible can become possible.

CHASE YOUR DREAM

In Memory of young Joseph and Thomas

And in dedication to all the youths of this world who are born afflicted with an illness and suffer each day of their life in pain.

Born under a lucky star . . .

The Master has put his angels in charge of us to watch over us wherever we go. (Ps. 91:11)

A thought . . .

The butterfly flies in the sky only after it learns to crawl on its belly.

CONTENTS

A Poem: Written by Jill Smoller, a friend

An Introduction

Part I: A Trip to Destiny
 Chapter: 1. Unaware Yet Of The Magic In The Air
          2. Nicknames
          3. A Common Bond
          4. Being Different . . . Is No Fun at All
          5. A Tilted Existence
          6. The Circle of Life
          7. The Beauty
          8. Spanky . . . The Missing Link
          9. The Drop Off
          10. Mom's Get-A-Way

Part II: The Twilight Zone
Chapter: 11. Busy Doing Nothing
         12. Roaring Snorts
         13. Born Under A Lucky Star
         14. Whistling A Happy Tune . . .
             With An Unhappy Smile
         15. Annie O'Hara . . . Mom
         16. Billy The Brat Strikes

Part III: Twinkle, Twinkle, Little Star
Chapter: 17. The Arrival of Hans Orion: The Starman
18. A Falling Star
19. Feeling Freaky
20. Jackson C. Pepperweather

Part IV: Hope For A Better Tomorrow
Chapter: 21. No Value in Being, A Goofy Little Kid
22. Death Mountain
23. Feeling-Down-Right-Dumpy Blue
24. A Letter to Santa
25. Hope for a Better Tomorrow
26. Simple Words With A Powerful Meaning
27. The Lesson of The Stable
28. A Wish on A Star
29. Reality of Imagination

Part V: A Christmas Adventure
Chapter: 30. A Wake-up Call From Above
31. The Bang On The Door
32. The First Step To Freedom,
The Sight of Light
33. An Unmistakable Grin
34. Silent Night - Holy Night
35. Listed Dead Or Alive

Part V: A Christmas Adventure - continued
Chapter: 36. Touched By A Smile
       37. A Need for Presence . . . Not Presents
       38. Whistling A Happy Tune . . . A Heavenly Sound
       39. Climbing the Mountain Called Death
       40. With A Crash . . . It Was Over

Part VI: A Temporary Stop Over - Stuck In a Holding Pattern
Chapter: 41. The Accident
       42. Billy Gets the Blame
       43. Having A Miserable Week
       44. Private Talks

Part VII: The Master Plan
Chapter: 45. Flying Upward into the Clouds
       46. The Tunnel of Life
       47. The Library
       48. The Throne of Glory
       49. Enter My Peace, Forever
       50. He Came To Serve - Not To Be Served

The Epilogue - The Riddles of God's Ways:
       Faith Is The Answer

A Poem
Written by Jill Smoller, a friend

I could feel the red ink
from your heart
as it trickled onto the pages.
So filled with a spirit
of life are your words
and the meaning delivered by sages.

And the snowman do dance
and our souls they do fly.
And wishes come true
in a dark, starless night.

I could see all the pain
and the joy
of this tapestry woven with love.
Magnificent colors
adoring us all and
the sharing of peace from above.

And the snowman do dance
and our souls they do fly.
And wishes come true
in a dark, starless night.

An Introduction:
Everything Was Created "In Love"...
Born Under A Lucky Star

God offers his peace and rest to all.
Everything was created in love . . . <u>Born Under
A Lucky Star</u>

PART I:
A Trip To Destiny

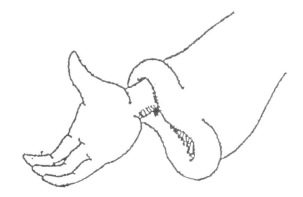

"Twas the night before Christmas (in the year 2000) when all through Emmitt Thomas Rhode's Cape Cod house not a creature was moving except, of course, good old J.C. Pepperweather..."

Chapter 1
Unaware Yet Of The Magic
In The Air

"Ahhh! Watch out, Ma!" Emmitt screamed, as the car skidded across the snow-covered lanes of the highway. Even in the backseat Emmitt could see that his Mom wasn't in complete control of the car.

"Whad'ya doin', Ma? You tryin' to get us killed on Christmas Eve?" Billy shouted. "Ya' barely missed that gasoline truck." Billy unlocked his seat belt and slid away from his brother, Emmitt, to get a better view. He peered over the front seat to see what was going on.

"The road is a sheet of ice below the snow. Billy, sit back! Now, mister! And put your seatbelt back on. We're sliding all over the place." Billy could see his Mom was scared. He sat back, but refused to put his seatbelt back on.

Gramps, sitting in the front seat, turned to his daughter and tried to calm her. "Annie, take a deep breath."

"Daddy, I'm scared! Look at me! My hands are shaking!"

3

"Come on, Annie, just keep it slow and steady and we'll be fine. Look!" Gramps pointed to an overhead road sign. "We're only a half a mile from the hospital. Get off here. But keep it slow. The exit ramp looks real slippery."

"Ma, the front window is all iced up! How can you see?" Emmitt watched nervously out of his window as the car veered off the highway. He wished his Mom would answer him. "Ma, watch out! Can't you see?! The cars are spinning out of control."

Mom gripped the steering wheel and swerved left, then right, missing a pile-up of smashed cars on both sides of the road. An inch closer to the left or right would have spelled disaster. Suddenly, she slammed on the brakes, screeched to a halt and crashed into a snow bank with a mighty bang. Billy went flying over the front seat and smacked into the dashboard. If only he had put his seatbelt on like his Mom had told him to do . . .

Dazed, Annie sat with her eyes closed, leaning her head on the wheel of the car. After a few seconds, she found the courage to speak. "Is everyone okay? Somebody please say something."

Billy was the first to speak as he looked up from under the dashboard with a bump protruding from his forehead. He tugged on his mother's coat. "My head hurts a little, but I think I'm okay. That was some nifty driving, Mom. Can we do it again?"

Annie looked down at her son in disbelief, shaking her head back and forth. "Are you crazy, Billy? Why wasn't your seatbelt on? You must have a loose screw jiggling in your brain. What is wrong with you? I mean, look at you. Your head's all scratched up. Here, put this tissue on your head to stop the bleeding. I'm so incredibly mad at you. Oh, my God, you could've killed yourself. You're grounded for the rest of your life. Now, get back in your seat, mister!"

"Don't get all bent out of shape, Mom." Billy lifted himself off the floor while holding the tissue to his head. "You make it sound like I was committing murder or something. I was just adjusting my seat belt, to make it tighter, you know."

4

"You watch your tongue, young man," Gramps scolded. "I'm tired of your pranks and lies." He helped Billy climb back into the backseat next to his brother who looked wobbly from the crash.

"How you doin', Emmitt?"

"I'm alright, Gramps. My heart is racing but I'm not hurt."

Gramps sighed with relief. "It's a miracle we didn't crash into any other cars." He looked at Annie when he said this. "Good thing our guardian angels weren't napping on us."

"You don't have to tell me, Dad." Annie took a deep breath to calm her shattered nerves. "But what do we do now?"

"Hopefully our angels are working the overtime shift." Gramps turned to look at the boys in the back seat. "I think we should just wait for help. What do you boys think?"

"Mom, I agree with Gramps," answered Emmitt. "But I think we should all go to the airport together to pick up Dad. It's probably going to be a while before we get plowed out. We're already late for my doctor's appointment. I wouldn't be surprised if he's stuck in the snow, too."

"Emmitt, don't pressure me - please. Let me calm down and collect myself. Look at my hands, for cryin' out loud, they're shaking all over the place."

"Jeepers creepers, Ma! I wasn't trying to cause any trouble. I just thought it was a good idea. Don't worry about it." But Emmitt was worried about it. The last thing he wanted to do was go to the hospital.

"Emmitt", said Gramps. "You did yourself proud today. You're now a hero like your Dad. He'll be proud of you for warning your mom like you did."

Emmitt noticed from the corner of his eye that Billy was secretly sticking his tongue at him. Emmitt ignored him as he usually did and smiled at his grandpa for making him feel better.

After a few seconds of silence, Gramps spoke again. "Emmitt, the people in the car crashes might need some help. Is it okay if Billy, Mom and I leave you alone for a couple minutes?"

"Sure, Gramps. Don't worry about me." After they left, Emmitt spent his time thinking as the car became cold and lonely. He sure wished he could join his family outside the car. But poor Emmitt couldn't do the ordinary things most people could.

★   ★   ★

Emmitt Thomas Rhodes usually enjoyed blizzards. But not tonight, in Bethlehem, Pennsylvania, where he grew up and lived.

For it was the night before Christmas,

the night before his 10th birthday,

and a night that was giving him the willy nillys.

Emmitt's favorite night of the whole year was being ruined by this terrible trip to the hospital. The only thing Emmitt wanted right now was the warmth of his house and the comfort of his best pal, Jackson C. Pepperweather. And who is Jackson C. Pepperweather? Why, he's a dog - the best dog a boy could have.

Emmitt gently scrubbed away the filmy fog covering the frozen car window. He looked out and searched the sky for the Christmas Star that had the power to grant him his Christmas wish. Emmitt was confused, though. He couldn't see anything in the sky. Why would the sky want to hide his Christmas Star? Emmitt hoped his Dad could help him answer this question later that night.

As the snow got higher and higher, Emmitt grew more and more worried. He wondered if Dad's plane would be able to land safely from a starless sky. Worse, Emmitt convinced himself that it was going to be another down right dumpy blue night.

But Emmitt was yet unaware of the magic in the air.

Chapter 2
Nicknames

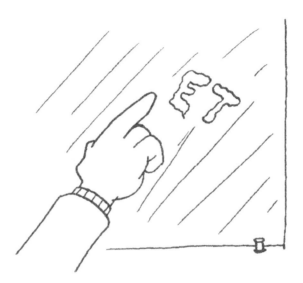

    Emmitt Thomas Rhodes drew his nickname on the car window, which had become foggy again. Emmitt liked his nickname. Everybody called him E.T., except his Mom, Dad and thirteen-year-old brother, Bubba Billy.
    Bubba liked to call Emmitt "E.R." because he was always going to the E.R., which stands for emergency room.
    Emmitt had to make regular visits to the hospital ever since he could remember. For poor Emmitt was born with a serious illness. He couldn't walk or run like normal kids.
    Emmitt hated going to the hospital. He often wondered if Bubba Billy knew how much he hated it. Emmitt wanted to cry when his big booger brother called him "E.R., the dummy-head loser."

Chapter 3
A Common Bond

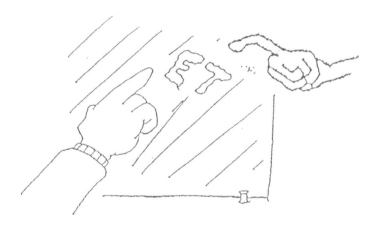

Emmitt liked being called E.T. because it was the same nickname used for that strange extra-terrestrial outer space creature in the movie.

Emmitt felt connected to the E.T. movie character because they both had strange and unusual appearances, and they both stuck out in the company of normal people. But Emmitt wished people would see beyond his differences, like they did with the movie character. Then maybe they would see that he was just like them.

Instead, normal people shied away from him because he looked funny. Emmitt often wondered what was stranger, the way he looked or the way people reacted to his strangeness.

Chapter 4
Being Different . . . Is No Fun at All

    Even though they were brothers, Bubba and Emmitt were very different. Billy was big like his father. Emmitt was small like . . . well, no one quite knows since he was adopted by the Rhodes' when he was just a little baby.
    Emmitt was a straight "A" student while Bubba struggled just to get a "C." The only class Bubba ever got an "A" in was gym.
    Emmitt read books to pass the time while Bubba spent all his free time watching TV and playing video games.
    Emmitt's favorite book was <u>A Christmas Carol</u> and his favorite character was Tiny Tim, the kindhearted cripple boy. Bubba's favorite movie was <u>Star Wars</u> and his favorite character was Darth Vader.
    But the biggest difference between the two was that Bubba could walk, run and have fun while E.T. had to move around in a wheelchair and needed help from others to get even the simplest things done.

Chapter 5
A Tilted Existence

    Emmitt hated that he couldn't walk. And he was always embarrassed when people would look at him like an alien creature from another world. He couldn't help it that his head was permanently tilted to the left side of his body, and his smile was off-center to the right side of his face. He just wished he could be like other people.
    Emmitt felt especially embarrassed when kids pointed or stared at him. Most of them were so scared by his looks that they couldn't even hide it.
    "What's wrong with you?" some kids would say. Or, "why do you look like a freak?" other kids would ask.

At least adults pretended not to notice. But not kids. That's why Emmitt didn't have friends of his own age. Except one. Her name was Lacey-Anne Ashley. She was his most special friend. But we'll get to her later.

Even when kids would conquer their fear and speak to Emmitt, he never knew how to react. He would get so flustered that anything he would say came out as gibberish. Then they would walk away. And Emmitt would be left to himself again.

To hide his shame, Emmitt hid in his home, much like the Beast in the movie <u>Beauty and the Beast</u>. At least at home he knew his family loved him. Maybe even by Bubba Billy. If he had to live a tilted existence as a lonely oddball, he'd rather do it at home. Yessiree.

But why did God make him this way?

Chapter 6
The Circle of Life

Emmitt couldn't understand his purpose in the circle of life. He wondered about the reason for his tilted existence. Why was he so odd? So strange? What could he possibly offer others?

Emmitt felt like running away. But he couldn't. He wasn't able to walk. Why couldn't he walk? Why did God make him so different? There were so many questions Emmitt couldn't answer.

He didn't want to be the best. He just wanted to fit-in, just a little bit. He just wanted to belong like everyone else. Was that too much to ask? He didn't dream more than what he needed, but he did need something more than he had. How could he fit in? If only he had legs that worked.

This is why Emmitt always wished and wished for something better. Everyday Emmitt prayed on a star for some answers.

Chapter 7
The Beauty

Emmitt Thomas Rhodes only had one friend in the whole world. Lacey-Anne Ashley. His special name for her was Spanky. She was the only person who could make Emmitt laugh. And she loved to call him E.T.

E.T. felt all giggly when Spanky was around because she made him laugh from the bottom of his tummy. He loved it when she raced him around the hallways of the hospital in his wheelchair like a race car.

Spanky was the bravest twelve-year-old tomboy. She could drop anyone with one of her right hooks, even butt-face Billy the brat. She had blond curly hair (when she had hair), round green eyes and a crooked smile that made her the cutest girl in the world.

Emmitt could talk to Spanky without stuttering because he felt completely at ease in her company. She treated him like any other kid. Everything seemed perfect when Spanky was around.

Chapter 8
Spanky . . .
The Missing Link

    When Spanky was around, she filled the big emptiness in Emmitt's life. She shared with him all her most secret secrets. Spanky told E.T. she was tired of all the aches and pains in her life. She wished for a day without hurt.

    Like E.T., Spanky was also different. Maybe that's why E.T. got along so well with Spanky. She was a regular at the hospital like Emmitt. Spanky had cancer. Despite her illness, Spanky was always ready to smile or laugh. Her positive attitude mirrored her beauty.

    Sometimes Spanky lost all her pretty hair, but she never complained or said it was unfair. However, Emmitt felt sad for Spanky because the medicine that was supposed to make her better often caused her to lose all of her strength and energy. He loved when she found energy to play with him but he loved her friendship the most.

Chapter 9
The Drop Off

"Holy-Moly! it's cold out here." Gramps shivered as he opened the car door. "How you makin' out back there, E.T.?"

"I'm fine, Gramps," E.T. responded. He did his best not to show his Grandpa that he was freezing. "Are the people in the cars hurt bad?"

"Yes, I'm afraid so." Gramps rubbed his hands together briskly, trying to warm them. "The good news is that the hospital ambulance got here quickly and everybody should be okay. Want to hear something really funny?"

"What's that?" wondered E.T.

15

"While your mother was explaining how the accident happened to police officer, Ed Riley -- you know, Billy's no-nonsense soccer coach?"

" Yeah, I know him, Gramps. He looks a little like the guy who played Forrest Gump in the movie."

"That's him," Gramps nodded. "Now listen to what your knucklehead brother did. This is the funny part. Billy somehow sneaks into Ed's police car and scares him half to death by turning on the siren. Ed nearly jumped out of his pants. You should'a seen the reaction on 'ol Ed. We didn't know what was funnier, Ed's reaction or Billy being handcuffed to the steering wheel. Well, that'll teach Billy to be a prankster." Gramps couldn't stop giggling.

"Wow, Billy must be in big trouble, huh, Gramps?"

"Not really. But I wish Ed would've thrown him in jail for a night. That boy needs some discipline. He's developing some real bad habits."

Emmitt pointed out the window, interrupting his grandfather. "Look! Isn't that Ma and Billy running towards the car?"

"Yup. Bob Bennett must've arrived with his tow truck. But I better get these windows cleaned off before your mother gets here. She'll have my hide if I don't. Hurry, hand me that ice scraper next to you."

Emmitt's mom shook her index finger at Gramps as she entered the car and started up the engine, which caused the chilly car to shutter with a clang. Gramps silently sneaked out of the car and began scraping the ice off the windows as the tow truck driver hooked the car up for the tow.

Gramps was shivering and his teeth were chattering as he stumbled back into the car. "Bob told me he's going to plow us out now. Boy, it's cold out there. But it sure feels good in here. Nice and warm."

"Good job on the windows, Dad. You're forgiven."

"Glad to be of service, my lady," Gramps smiled. "Annie, can you please grant your old father one favor on Christmas Eve?"

"Anything you want. Your wish is my command."

16

"Please drive slowly to the hospital. I don't think I could handle any more excitement tonight." Gramps chuckled and began to sing jingle bells to the music on the radio.

But Emmitt was feeling downright dumpy blue because after a few minutes they arrived at the entrance of the hospital. It was a dungeon of horror for Emmitt, a place of pain and sadness. Emmitt knew the excitement and joy of Christmas Eve was going to vanish when he entered the hospital emergency room.

"Mom, I'm feeling sick. I don't wanna go to the hospital. Can we please change our plans just this one time? I wanna go and pick up Dad with you. Please?"

To everyone's surprise, Billy agreed with his brother. "Mom, my creepy brother, and your creepy son, happens to be right this one time. The hospital is no place to celebrate Christmas. We should stay together as a family tonight."

Emmitt's Mom stopped the car at the curb of the hospital entrance. She looked across the front seat at Gramps and pleaded with her eyes for him to help her out.

Gramps turned his head to face his grandsons in the back seat before he spoke. "Well, boys, unfortunately this is what we got. Doctor Clarence is going away on vacation tomorrow and he gave me strict orders to bring Emmitt in for an examination. He wants to know why E.T.'s left leg hurts so badly. I wish it was otherwise, but we have no choice. We have to see the doctor today." Gramps turned to his daughter and shrugged his shoulders. "I guess it's time to say good luck. Sweetheart, be careful."

"Promise. Good thing the airport's only five miles away. It can't be that bad." But Mom didn't sound so confident. "Now get your butt out of my car, Dad. It's already five fifty and Emmitt's appointment was scheduled for four o'clock."

Mom looked sternly and shook her finger at Billy as he opened the car door to leave. "I'm warning you, Mister. Behave yourself. Don't forget your Dad's coming home tonight."

17

"I'll be good, Mom. Promise." Billy gave Mom a hasty kiss good-bye. "I'll watch after Gramps and Emmitt. Don't ya' worry about nothin'." Billy said this as he ran away from the car and vanished into the blanket of snowflakes falling from the sky.

Meanwhile, Gramps lifted Emmitt out of the car and into his wheelchair. Emmitt waved good-bye to his Mom as Gramps pushed him carefully across the icy entrance ramp to the emergency room.

Emmitt and Gramps entered the hospital, followed by Billy. "Gramps, I feel crummy." Emmitt said. "I hate when mom leaves me. And I hate it even more when I'm away from J.C. Pepperweather."

Gramps patted Emmitt on the shoulder and sighed. "I know just how you feel," he said, "I hate when your mother leaves me too. But don't you worry, kiddo, we'll be home soon enough. Don't forget, you might be able to see Spanky tonight."

Emmitt's face lit up with anticipation.

Chapter 10
Mom's Get-A-Way

Emmitt, Billy and Gramps looked through the windows and watched Mom's gas guzzling, oil leaking, red station wagon plow through the slush and ice.

"Gramps, do you want to hear my 'Star-Trek' nickname for Mom's car?" asked Emmitt.

Gramps shook his chin up and down. "Sure, what is it?"

"THE STARSHIP ENTER slowly - it's no PRIZE!"

Gramps laughed at Emmitt's wit.

"Yo, Gramps," interrupted Billy. "Nothing stops mom, huh! She's not afraid of anythin'. Not even a blizzard. She's s-o-o-o cool, huh!"

Gramps smiled at Billy. "You're absolutely right, Billy! She's one brave cookie monster. Don't you worry about her. She'll be all right out there."

Emmitt tugged on Gramps coat sleeve to get his attention. "Hey Gramps, tell me the truth. Do you think we'll be stuck here all night on Christmas Eve?" Emmitt was handicapped but he was no fool. He knew that the bad road conditions would delay Mom's return to the hospital.

"I don't know for sure, E.T., but let's hope for the best and think good thoughts. Can you do that for me?"

Emmitt shook his head. "Sure can, Gramps." Immediately Emmitt thought of Spanky. When he did, he couldn't help but smile. "Gramps, I'm thinkin' good thoughts and I'm startin' to feel a whole lot better."

Gramps looked down at his grandson. "I see you've found something to be happy about. I wonder if it isn't a blonde-haired girl." Emmitt smiled up at Gramps. "That's good, E.T., hold on to what makes you happy. Because when you do, life becomes more fun."

Part II
The Twilight Zone

Chapter 11
Busy Doing Nothing

Even on Christmas Eve there was a line at the front desk. Emmitt, Billy and Gramps had no choice but to wait with everyone else until their turn arrived. As Emmitt looked around the room, all he saw were unhappy faces. Some moaned in pain, some sat silently, some looked anxious. But one thing was for sure, they all looked liked they would rather be home in front of a warm fire.

It wasn't long before Nurse Petersen spotted Emmitt, Billy and Gramps from across the hall. She was the last person E.T. wanted to see. She was the crankiest person in the whole world. And she was always yelling, like she was doing right now. "Everybody just calm down! You'll get your turn soon enough! I better not hear any complaints!" she screamed. Her yelling seemed to cause more disorder than order.

23

She moved in a turtle like fashion as she approached Emmitt, huffing and puffing all the way. "What's your problem? You're late and now you don't want to wait like everybody else! I'm tired and grouchy so don't moan or groan to me about anything. My replacement is stuck in the snow so you're not the only ones who have to be here on Christmas Eve! If you people were more careful and didn't injure yourselves, I wouldn't have to be here!" It seemed Nurse Petersen didn't care about anyone but herself. "Just grab a chair and chill out! It's not my fault the doctor's late! So stop your complaining!"

Gramps wheeled E.T. off the line. "Oh boy, we didn't say a word and she still blasted us," said Gramps shaking his head. "She's a cranky one, all right, but we should feel sorry for her because people like her waste their life caring about no one," Gramps whispered.

"I kinda feel sorry for her, Gramps," Emmitt sympathized. "It seems as if she doesn't care about anyone, and nobody seems to care about her. She must be a real lonely lady. What do think, Gramps?"

Gramps nodded his agreement.

"I'm startin' to feel sad for us, too. The last thing I wanted was to be stranded in a hospital on Christmas Eve. Do you think the doctor's stuck in the snow somewhere?" asked Emmitt.

"Probably," answered Gramps. "But don't get too upset over it. Let's make the best out of a bad situation. C'mon, we'll go over to our favorite spot next to the window. Then I can take a nap."

Chapter 12
Roaring Snorts

Gramps pushed E.T.'s wheelchair away from the noise of the front desk to a window overlooking the rolling hills of the hospital grounds. Powerful spotlights shining from the hospital roof lit up the whole hospital landscape. Gramps was thrilled. "Falling snow is a restful sight. Doesn't it just make you want to snuggle in your blankets?"

"Sure does, Gramps. Why do I love this spot so much?" asked E.T.

"Good feelings come from good thoughts, Emmitt. I have no idea why you would get good feelings from this spot, since it's smack in the middle of the emergency room you call the *dungeon of horror*. But don't lose your good feelings. Sometimes that's all we got."

Gramps turned his attention back to the confusion of the emergency room. "Where'd your brother go?"

Emmitt looked around the room. "I don't know, Gramps, but I bet he's up to no good. Are ya' gonna look for him?"

"I'm getting too old to chase after your brother. All I'm concerned about right now is my nap." Gramps crawled to a chair near the window and sat down, yawning. He smiled to Emmitt with his usual comforting grin, gave a familiar wacky wink of the eye, and began snoring in no time.

A woman sitting next to Gramps smiled at Gramps' rhythmic snorting. "He sounds like a trombone," she said to Emmitt. She giggled, unable to contain her laughter. Emmitt giggled with her.

Meanwhile, Billy disappeared from sight. Emmitt figured Billy was up to no good, and when Billy was in search of trouble, it always found him with a capital T. Since Emmitt couldn't do anything to stop Billy from carrying out his mission of no good, he decided to just lean back in his chair and wait for Billy to strike. After all, it was a waiting room.

Chapter 13
Born Under A Lucky Star

Emmitt searched the skies. There was no sign of his lucky star. Mom always called Emmitt her special little man. She told him he was special because he was born under a lucky star on Christmas, like another special boy who was also born on Christmas in Bethlehem.

But Emmitt didn't feel special tonight. His star was hiding in a starless sky. He wished it would appear. He wished it again and again, because Emmitt didn't know if a wish could be granted in a starless sky.

Emmitt looked at his pocket-watch. It read six thirty five.

Suddenly, Nurse Petersen started yelling. "Everybody quiet down! Whaddayou think this is, a circus?"

She was a riot trying to stop a riot, Emmitt thought.

Chapter 14
Whistling A Happy Tune...
With An Unhappy Smile

Gramps' snoring was the loudest noise in the noisy room. It was so loud that it caught Nurse Petersen's attention. She kept looking over to him with a mean look. Emmitt looked away in case she decided to throw mean looks at him. He tried to think good thoughts instead of Nurse Petersen's nasty looks. Eventually his thoughts settled on his Gramps.

Gramps was fun, smart, a best pal and a great storyteller. He was a huge man with soft hands, with a big stomach and a gentle heart. He occasionally missed weekly church services but he never missed a chance to say a kind word to anyone he met whether friend or stranger. He never judged or talked about others. That's why everyone in town liked Gramps.

Gramps was simply an honest man who never pointed a finger at others when they made a mistake. He wasn't perfect, but most people thought of him as a holy man.

28

Gramps was always smiling or whistling a happy tune. The only time Gramps lost his happy smile was when Grandma Katherine died. That was the saddest day in Gramps' life. Emmitt never forgot how much Gramps cried. And he never wanted to see him so sad again. Emmitt loved him too much to see him unhappy.

Emmitt loved Grandma Katherine, too. He thought of her every time he thought about Gramps, he couldn't separate the two. He missed the quiet nights when he read books aloud to her while she knitted in her rocker. She always had words of wisdom to offer him, especially about the value of reading books. "You are wise beyond your age, my little bookworm, because you read well and often. People who seldom read or rarely listen to the viewpoint of others' have *w-i-s-d-u-m-b*, not wisdom." She spelled her make believe word for lack of wisdom. "Don't be dumb! Be smart like your mother. Your mother read for many years before she began to write her own books. Her wisdom has touched many hearts."

Grandma Katherine was an elegant, refined English lady, so unlike her daughter, Annie, E.T.'s Mom.

Chapter 15
Annie O'Hara . . . Mom

Only Billy and Emmitt had the privilege of calling their mother Mom.

Everyone else in town called her Annie O'Hara, even though her married name was Annie Rhodes. Some things just took time to change in a small town like Bethlehem.

Gramps' special name for his only child - his Irish lassie - was "Shamrock Rosy." She was his rosy-hair lucky charm.

Annie was a mirror image of her mother in looks, but was different than her in many ways. Grandma Katherine was stately, a lady who dressed in silk and lace, whereas Annie was a bubbly, freckle faced, happy-go-lucky free spirit who liked to dress down in denim jeans and baggy sweaters.

Annie had a child-like attitude that all things were possible, and firmly believed that everyone could attain success if they just tried. She was a dreamer chaser; full of nervous energy that radiated a ray of sunshine to anyone she met. Annie O'Hara was different than E.T.'s grandma, but she was 'grand' too.

Chapter 16
Billy The Brat Strikes

    Luigi, the short and chubby hospital janitor, stood on his empty water bucket and shouted to all the chattering voices in the waiting room. "Hush, everyone!"
    Luigi's shout woke Gramps. It also brought the attention of Nurse Petersen, who quickly entered the waiting room to let Luigi know she didn't care for anyone shouting except her.
    "What is your problem?!" shouted Nurse Petersen. "I do the yellin' around here, not you, Luigi!"
    Luigi cringed under her stare. You can tell he regretted shouting. No one liked to look directly at Nurse Petersen. She had a nasty mole on her chin and a big hooknose that made her look like the wicked witch from the Wizard of Oz. Anyone would cringe at the sight of her.
    With his eyes firmly fixed on the floor, Luigi finally found the courage to speak up. He did so with a thick Italian accent. "Who-a, took-a, my, broom-a? Moma- mia, I need-a my broom-a. I got-a gett-a my work-a don-a som-a tim-a tonight-a."

31

Suddenly, Billy appeared and broke the uncomfortable silence with a yell. "Yo, mister, I found your broom-a!"

Emmitt looked across the room at Billy and realized that someone had left the janitor's broom on Nurse Petersen's chair. A note was hanging off the broom handle.

Billy ripped the note from the broom and read the note aloud. "Dear Nurse Petersen," he began. "I'm bewitched by your presence. Please fly away with me to Oz. Your admirer."

The room erupted in laughter. No one could stop laughing. Nurse Petersen bowed her head in shame and waddled out of the room. She was too embarrassed to look at anyone.

"It looks like the work of Billy-the-brat," E.T. whispered to Gramps.

"It was a cruel prank, even for Billy," answered Gramps.

E.T. and Gramps were the only ones who didn't laugh in the room. Emmitt knew too well how it felt when people made fun of him. Emmitt felt sad for her and shared her hurt. He wished he could give her a hug.

PART III
Twinkle, Twinkle Little Star

Chapter 17
The Arrival of Hans Orion:
The Starman

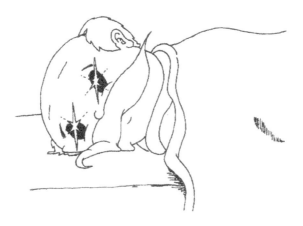

"E.T., you'll have to excuse me for a moment." Gramps rose sluggishly from his chair. He looked hot-piping mad. "Someone's gotta put some sense into your knuckle-head brother. He can't keep going around hurting people." Gramps walked out of the waiting room with his familiar limp, shaking his head back and forth in anger.

Just as Emmitt was about to snooze, a loud, blaring ambulance siren woke him up. A second later, an odd looking man, the height of a stickball bat and weighing about 75 pounds, rolled in on a stretcher, carried by two medics.

Emmitt looked at the unusual creature lying on the stretcher. Something about the man made Emmitt feel wonderful. Perhaps it was the gleeful glow gleaming gently from the stranger's eyes. Whatever it was, it removed all the unease in E.T. A calm and peace unlike anything Emmitt had ever experienced suddenly washed over him. He felt so safe being in the same room with him. Could this funny looking creature be his Starman sent down from heaven?

Suddenly, the stranger spoke to him from across the noisy room as if they were alone. The stranger's voice seemed to drown all the other voices. "Close your eyes, E.T., and take comfort in my voice. My friends call me Hans Orion. And I came here to see you. I work for M.A.N., which stands for Master's Angel Network. I'm going to be your own personal guardian angel, E.T."

Emmitt snapped out of his dreamlike trance as soon as the medics starting moving the funny little man to the examination room. Emmitt sat with his jaw wide open wondering whether he had hallucinated. He couldn't believe that his answer to his wish on a lucky star had come true. The only thing Emmitt was certain about now was the stranger's name. Hans Orion. It fit the little man like a perfect glove. Emmitt knew something special was happening. He felt like running around and giving everyone a hug. But he couldn't run. Or walk. All he could do was wheel around. But at this moment he didn't care. Hans Orion had arrived! Just imagine, my own personal guardian angel, Emmitt thought.

Chapter 18
A Falling Star

Police Sergeant Ed Riley, covered head to toe with snow, ran into the waiting room. "Can somebody help me? I'm looking for the ambulance medics!"

"Grab a chair and chill out! They're in the examination room," Nurse Petersen replied.

Sergeant Riley turned and gave Nurse Petersen an unkind look as he brushed snow off his clothes. Sergeant Riley was an impatient man and the wait was frustrating him. He paced back and forth in the emergency room like a caged lion, tapping his pen against his head as he watched the seconds pass by.

Emmitt rolled his wheelchair towards the police officer. He wanted to know more about Hans Orion. But Officer Riley wouldn't tell anything to Emmitt, at least not until he had a chance to speak to Hans Orion himself.

37

Five minutes passed before the two medics returned to the waiting room. Officer Riley wasted no time drilling them with questions. "What happened? And don't you be leaving anything out. I wanna know everything."

"Hard to explain, officer. I mean, even if I told you, you'd probably think I was crazy or something," replied the younger of the two medics. "We found the guy in a field lying face up. He was wearing a white shepherd's robe and sandals. That's it. No jacket, or scarf or even socks. I mean, it's like he fell from the sky. There weren't even any footprints. You figure it out."

Billy and Gramps entered the waiting room and sat down next to Emmitt just as the medics were leaving. Tears were streaming down Billy's cheeks.

Gramps leaned over to Emmitt and whispered in his ear. "Billy is such a coward. He won't admit to the broom prank and refuses to apologize to Nurse Petersen. Wait till your Dad finds out about this." Gramps gazed up at Officer Riley standing next to him then turned back to Emmitt. "What happened? What's Sergeant Riley doing here at the hospital?"

"He's trying to figure out how someone got injured. The medics brought in an old man who looked half-dazed. Know what I think, Gramps?" Emmitt spoke loud enough for Officer Riley to hear. "I think my Starman fell down from heaven to answer my Christmas wish."

Sergeant Riley laughed when he heard E.T. "Perhaps that's how it really happened, son, but my chief would chew off my ear if I told him that." The policeman bent down and looked Emmitt straight in the eyes as he spoke with a frown on his face. "Since I have to write up an accident report tonight, do you by chance know the name of your Starman?"

Emmitt smiled proudly and announced, "Hans Orion! And he works for M.A.N! which stands for. . ."

"Alright, I've heard enough," interrupted Sergeant Riley. "I'm outta here. If you say his name's Hans Orion, that's good enough for me. Thanks for your help, kid." Officer Riley left, shaking his head in disbelief.

Suddenly, Emmitt sat forward in his wheelchair with a creeping feeling. His father, Captain Rhodes, a pilot in the U.S. Air Force, was scheduled to land his supersonic jet from the same starless sky that Hans Orion fell from just a short time ago. What if he couldn't land safely and fell just like Hans Orion? What if he crashed? These thoughts swirled in Emmitt's head until Ms. Maddy interrupted his thoughts with her booming voice.

"E.T.? Where are you, boy? Doctor Clarence just arrived and he's waitin' for you in examination room number Two A. You know he doesn't like to be kept waitin'! Now let me help ya get in there!"

Ms. Maddy was the nickname for Nurse Matilda. She was a big cheerful Jamaican woman with a thick accent. Everybody liked her, including Emmitt.

Emmitt looked at his pocket-watch, which read six fifty-five P.M.

Chapter 19
Feeling Freaky

Ms. Maddy got behind Emmitt's wheelchair and grabbed the handles. She spoke to Gramps. "I'll wheel Master Emmitt to the examination room if yer promise to keep a mindful eye on yer other boy. God knows that boy needs lookin' afta'."

Gramps grinned at Ms. Maddy. She sure knew Billy. As they left, Gramps placed his hand solidly behind Billy's neck and twisted it until his head turned and they were face to face. "I'm warning you, Billy. If you pull another prank, I'll ring your hooligan neck!" Gramps released his grip on Billy with one hand as he turned and waved goodbye to Emmitt with the other.

Ms. Maddy pushed Emmitt to the doctor's office. "What's wrong, boy?" Ms. Maddy asked. "Why yer lookin' so troubled? Yer can tell Ms. Maddy, Emmitt. Yer know I always listen to you."

"Ms. Maddy," Emmitt began. "Those two dorky student-doctors that work with Doctor Clarence always hurt me. They practice on me, you know. They stretch and jerk my legs like I'm a doll or something." Emmitt looked over his shoulder to see if Ms. Maddy understood. "I'd complain to Doctor Clarence, but he'd just smile and tell me to relax."

40

"Don't yer worry yourself any. I promise yer that they're not goin' to hurt yer any with me aroun'. I'm not goin' to leave yer side until the doctor's done with yer and I bring yer back to yer grandpa."

"Thanks, Ms. Maddy. You're the best nurse I ever had." Emmitt spotted Doctor Clarence and the two student doctors standing at the end of the long hallway. With Ms. Maddy at his side, he wasn't as afraid as he usually was. "Ms. Maddy, do ya wanna know Billy's nickname for the Doctor?"

Matilda looked down at Emmitt and smiled as she whispered in his ear. "It better not be rude."

"Naw. It's just funny. Billy likes to call Doc Clarence the Nutty Professor because he acts a little nutty when he tells his corny jokes." Emmitt pointed to the Doctor. "I mean, he does look a little nutty, don't ya think? Look at his curly hair. It's all messy like a mop. And look at the clothes he wears - plaid jacket and red bow tie. No one in their right mind wears such things."

Nurse Matilda tried not to laugh as she wheeled Emmitt into examination room number Two A. Now that she thought about it, Dr. Clarence did look like the Nutty Professor.

"What's so funny?" he asked. "The jokes on me if you don't share it."

"Okay Doc, you wanna hear a nutty joke?" asked Emmitt.

"Sure," replied Dr. Clarence.

"Why did the nutty squirrel climb the tree?"

"Why?"

"He wanted to act like a nut."

Dr. Clarence laughed and immediately shot back with a joke of his own. "E.T., why did the turtle with a belly-ache cross the road?"

"Why?"

"To find the shell station because he felt a little gassy."

Emmitt laughed. "That's a good one, Doc. It's nutty like you."

41

Dr. Clarence walked away from Emmitt to talk to Nurse Matilda. "Ms. Maddy, I know how busy it is tonight; if you have to leave, I will surely understand."

Nurse Matilda looked at her watch before replying. "That's alright, Doc. I know it's busy and gettin' late, but I promised my little friend here I would keep an eye on em'. Yer know he's a little afraid because yer all hurt him sometimes. So you be gentle with him or I'll have ta' whip yer hide."

Dr. Clarence smiled. "Well, then we'll just have to be extra careful with Emmitt here. Hey, E.T.," Doctor Clarence turned and stepped back towards Emmitt. "Do you want to play a knock-knock game?"

"Sure, Doc."

"Knock! Knock!"

"Who's there?"

"Pat."

"Pat who?"

"Pat me on the shoulder if anyone hurts you. Is that a deal?" Dr. Clarence held out his hand for Emmitt to shake.

Emmitt shook it with a big smile. "It's a deal, Doc!"

Doctor Clarence began his examination by reading Emmitt's medical chart aloud. He thoroughly explained to the students all the medical reasons for Emmitt's illness before he examined him.

Emmitt suddenly felt like a freak at a sideshow. Each student agreed with everything the Nutty Professor said with a nod, as if they were going to be graded.

Emmitt decided to ignore the doctors. He wanted to forget that he was different. He wanted to imagine a better world where he could fight dragons and rescue maidens. Then he thought of his pal, Jackson C. Pepperweather.

Chapter 20
Jackson C. Pepperweather

    The thought of his pup, Jackson Clyde Pepperweather, brought a smile to Emmitt's face, and for a short while took his mind off the check-up.

    Dad liked to call Jackson "J.C. the P.P. Pup" because whenever he got excited he would always wet Mom's favorite carpet, which was usually the beige one in the living room. Even though Mom would yell at him, she always forgave him afterwards. Emmitt, on the other hand, never yelled at Jackson C. Pepperweather because he loved him too much. After all, Jackson never made fun of him or called him names. And he would always lick his face in greeting. If only everyone could love people the way Jackon C. Pepperweather did.

    The doctor shook Emmitt, startling him from his loving thoughts of J.C. Pepperweather. "Your check-up is over Master Rhodes." The doctor glanced over to Nurse Matilda and then at the clock on the wall. "Ms. Maddy, please do me a big favor?"

    "Well, that all depends, Doctor," replied Nurse Maddy.

"Ask Mr. O'Hara to join me in the doctor's lounge in five minutes. I want to speak to him briefly about E.T. before I go back out into that blizzard."

"Yer got it, boss."

The Nutty Professor gave Emmitt a smile before he disappeared behind a curtain.

"Nurse Maddy, where did the doctor go?" asked Emmitt.

"No idea. Knowing him, he could be anywhere."

"Not even a good-bye. I think it's kinda rude, don't ya' think?" Emmitt asked.

Nurse Matilda began to wheel him out of the exam room. "You right about that, Master Emmitt."

E.T. wished J.C. Pepperweather was around to brighten his spirits on this jolly-less Christmas Eve.

PART IV
Hope For A Better Tomorrow

Chapter 21
No Value in Being,
A Goofy Little Kid

Nurse Matilda wheeled Emmitt to his favorite window, stopping him at his special spot next to Gramps and Billy in the jammed waiting room.

"Welcome back, son!" said Gramps. He patted him gently on his shoulder. "How'd you make out?"

Nurse Matilda spoke before Emmitt had a chance to answer. "Mr. O'Hara, yer grandson did himself proud today and I made double sure those student-doctors didn't hurt yer boy any." Nurse Matilda beamed with a self-satisfied grin. "And the doctor wants to speak to yer in the doctor's lounge. Now hurry yerself along. He's in a hurry, yer know. If yer don't hurry up, you might miss 'em. He never stays in one spot long enough, God knows."

"Ms. Maddy, you are the kindest nurse a patient can have." With that Gramps kissed her on the cheek. "You're a Christmas presence every day of the year."

"Mr. O'Hara, yer sure are an old sweet talker and yer makin' this girl blush like a young maiden." And blush she did. Nurse Matilda slowly strolled away, not even noticing Nurse Peterson at the front desk, who gave her a frazzled look, probably wondering what could make a person so happy.

Gramps limped out of the waiting room. Emmitt only had to wait five minutes before he reappeared. He carried three donuts and a cup of hot coffee with him. "I have some good news to report," said Gramps. He sat down and handed Emmitt and Billy a donut.

"The doctor believes that the pain in your leg is nothing more than growing pains. That means you're getting bigger. So there's nothing to worry about. The pain should disappear any day now. And he wishes you a happy birthday and a Merry Christmas. Best part, we have clearance from the good doctor to go home and celebrate Christmas."

Despite the good news, Emmitt wasn't so happy. "Then why didn't the doctor give the good news to both of us?"

Billy answered Emmitt's question before Gramps had a chance to respond. "Because you're just a nobody. Gramps pays the bill, so he gets to speak to the Nutty Professor – not you! You're just one patient out of hundreds. What doctor would care about you? Now you understand, numnut?"

Emmitt was too shocked to speak. Billy's words hit Emmitt in the chest with the force of a hundred hurtling baseballs. As much as he tried, Emmitt couldn't stop the tears from pouring out of his eyes. He wished so much his brother didn't hate him. *Why, Billy, why do you always have to be so mean, Emmitt thought.* He couldn't help but look to his Grandfather for help.

48

"Who the heck do you think you are, Billy! You don't speak to your brother that way! Never! You got me, mister!" Gramps was too angry to say anymore. He had to take several deep breaths before he could continue. "One of these days, I have a mind to whip your behind with my belt. You can't keep going around saying such hateful things to people. And to your brother of all people. He's got feelings too, you know."

Billy hated when his Gramps yelled at him. "Aw, Gramps, you know I was just joking. But E.R. always asks the dumbest questions. Why do you always answer him?"

Gramps was doing everything he could to control his temper. "Listen, Billy, let's play a little game, alright?"

"Sure. What do I have to do?"

"All you have to do is listen closely and think carefully. Can you do that for me?"

"I'll give it a shot." Billy responded slowly, which didn't convince Gramps that he wanted to play this game.

"Would you agree that Doctor Clarence is one of the richest men in this town?" asked Gramps.

"Yeah."

"And would you also agree that Doctor Clarence doesn't need Emmitt as a patient?"

"I guess so."

"Then why would Doctor Clarence come out in this blizzard, possibly risk an accident, just to see your brother?"

"Because he won't get paid unless he does?"

"Do you really think that? Do you honestly think the Doctor traveled all the way to the hospital on Christmas Eve just to make money? Come on, Billy. You can do better than that."

Billy was stumped. He sat for a while and tried to think why indeed the good doctor would risk so much just to see a sick boy. He knew it couldn't just be for the money. After a few minutes of thinking, the answer came to him. But he didn't like the answer. "What are you sayin', Dr. Clarence really cares about Emmitt?"

"You tell me. It's your answer." Gramps stared at Billy without blinking. He wanted so much for Billy to believe in the goodness of others.

Billy could see that his grandfather was serious. He thought about his answer for a while. He couldn't help but feel that Dr. Clarence really did care about Emmitt. "Alright, Gramps, I give in. It's obvious Dr. Clarence didn't come here for the money. So it's gotta be because he cares. Are you happy, now?"

Gramps gave Billy a smile. "There's hope for you yet, my boy."

"I guess it's better to think before I speak, huh?"

"That's what I've been telling you for years. Maybe it's finally starting to sink into that thick head of yours."

Billy was happy that his grandfather wasn't so angry with him. He loved his grandfather too much not to listen to him. But he knew his grandfather wouldn't truly be happy with him until he apologized.

"Gramps, I'm real sorry about all the trouble I've caused. I'll try harder not to lose my temper from now on. You got my word on it."

"Good boy, Billy. And I'm gonna hold you to your promise."

As Gramps and Billy smiled at each other, Emmitt waited patiently for an apology from his brother. But one never came. He wished so much his brother would love him as much as he loved him. *How could Billy be so rotten and mean, Emmitt thought.*

An uneventful hour passed by before Emmitt heard Nurse Petersen's blaring voice over the noise in the room. "Mr. O'Hara, please come to the front desk. You have a phone call from your daughter. It's on line three."

Gramps stood up and looked down at Emmitt with his fingers crossed. "Say a prayer for good news."

50

    "I got a bad feeling about this call, Gramps." But Emmitt crossed his fingers anyway. "I keep thinking my lucky star is hiding on me tonight."

    Emmitt watched nervously as Gramps limped to the telephone. He prayed to his Star for good news. But the nagging feeling that bad news was on its way would not leave him.

    Gramps walked back from his telephone call. Something in his walk, perhaps the way he was dragging his feet, told Emmitt that his feelings were confirmed. Gramps sat down, shook his head, and shrugged his shoulders.

    Emmitt could barely contain himself. His voice trembled as he spoke. "Gramps, tell me everything's okay. Please tell me Dad's safe."

    "Boys, your Dad's plane skidded on the runway," Gramps began.

    Emmitt and Billy's eyes went wide with fear.

    Before they could utter a word, Gramps put up his hands. "But it stopped a few-yards from the end of the runway. He's safe. Your Mother's with him as I speak."

    Both boys exhaled in relief, not even realizing they had been holding their breaths.

    "The bad news is the roads are closed for the night. That means your parents are stuck at the airport."

    Emmitt and Billy covered their mouths with their hands, too upset to speak. They couldn't imagine a Christmas without Mom and Dad being present. Tears began to fill their eyes.

Chapter 22
Death Mountain

Bubba jumped out of his chair and stormed away.

"Where you going, Billy?" Gramps asked.

"I'm going outside. I'm tired of being cooped up in here."

Gramps realized that Billy needed to be by himself. Maybe some fresh air will help him to calm down. "Be careful! It's real icy out there. My weak heart can't take anymore excitement tonight." Gramps watched Billy walk away.

Emmitt turned to Gramps as Billy disappeared from sight. "I think Billy hates me. I mean, he blames me for everything that goes wrong in his life."

Gramps looked at Emmitt with an understanding look. "Oh, Emmitt, your brother doesn't hate you. Don't ever think that. He gets angry at you because you have something that he can't have."

Emmitt stared at his grandfather with a puzzled look. "Don't be silly, Gramps. What could I possibly have that he would want?"

52

"Attention!" Gramps shouted. As he let Emmitt think this over, he took out his pipe. "Billy resents all the attention you get. I think he sometimes feels like a forgotten part of the family. What do you think Emmitt? Do you think he could get angry with you for that reason?"

Emmitt scratched his head and shrugged his shoulders. He didn't know if his Gramps was being serious.

"Ever notice that Billy becomes the prankster only when he feels no one's paying attention to him?" Gramps began to clean his pipe with a tissue. "I think Billy gets himself in trouble just to draw attention away from you, even if he has to get punished to do so."

"Wait a second. Are you sayin' that Billy feels left out because I need extra help from Mom, Dad and you?"

"That's exactly what I'm saying, Emmitt."

"Gee, since you put it that way, I can understand why Billy acts out so much. Then he really doesn't hate me?"

"I think we've already answered that."

Emmitt smiled at the knowledge that his brother just wanted to be loved as much as he did.

Gramps put his pipe in his mouth and started chewing on it as he continued to speak to Emmitt. "But knowing why Billy acts as he does is only half the battle. To win the war you have to figure out a way to make Billy stop."

"But I can't! If I make him mad for any reason, he teases me until I start to cry."

"You have to understand that Billy only cares about his own feelings right now because he feels hurt himself." Gramps looked into Emmitt's eyes. "But what's the best way to make Billy feel that he's not being ignored?"

"I don't know, Gramps. Do you have a plan?"

Gramps nodded. "Do you want to hear it?"

"Absolutely! What's the plan?"

"There are two parts to my one plan; but God knows I don't know which part goes first. That's going to be your call but remember both are equally important." Emmitt sat up in his chair and listened attentively. "Billy needs attention. So ask him to help you with something. If he helps, just think how grateful everybody would be that he was so helpful. You'd make him a hero. You'd give him all the attention he's been wanting. What do you think so far?"

"Gramps, that sounds like a good idea. What's the other part?"

"The second part will be much harder for you to carry out. You'll have to eat some crow before the turkey trimmings can be served."

Emmitt's eyes shot open. "Gramps, what in the world are you telling me to do?"

Gramps chuckled. "Apologizing to your brother even though you didn't do anything wrong is called eating crow, my boy. Catch your brother off guard and see him wiggle like a fish out of water."

"Do you really think I can outwit the big jerk?"

"Yes! And I think the plan works because Billy needs to be shown forgiveness to learn how to forgive. I believe he will show you kindness if you show kindness to him first."

"I don't know, Gramps." Emmitt thought hard about what his Grandfather told him. "I don't know if a dummy-head loser like me can pull it off."

"I don't ever want to hear you say that about yourself, you hear me!" Gramps looked sternly at Emmitt. "You are not a loser. The only losers I know are the ones who don't try in life. Ever since you were born, you've been struggling harder than anybody I know. That makes you a winner."

Emmitt didn't like it when his Grandfather yelled at him. But he was so proud that his Grandfather thought he was a winner. "Do you really think I'm a winner?"

"Absolutely. Even though you can't walk or run, you never complain or ask for pity. That makes you a winner in my book."

54

"Thanks, Gramps. I love you for making me feel special. I think I'll give your plan a shot."

"That a boy. And remember, even though you may think Billy owes you an apology, it is more important that you forgive him. The strength of a man is judged not by his ability to apologize, but by his ability to forgive. Anyone can apologize. But only heroes can forgive. Be a hero, Emmitt. Just remember what Grandma Katherine used to say. *A spoonful of forgiveness and kindness will cure a bucket full of anger and hate.* She lived her whole life believing that. If it worked for her, it can work for you."

Emmitt looked through the window as he thought about what his Grandfather just said. Suddenly, he noticed Billy grab a sleigh from a little boy. "Oh know, Gramps! Billy's at it again!"

Gramps looked through the window. "Drat that boy! He's not only a brat, but he's big bully to boot!"

Emmitt and Gramps sat motionless as Billy climbed what the kids in town called *Death Mountain.* It wasn't really a mountain but a big hill. All the kids wanted to ride a sleigh down this steep, slippery, snowy peak. It was the supreme test of courage for any kid in this town.

Gramps and Emmitt watched Bubba huff and puff his way up to the top of the mountain with the *borrowed* sled. Billy spotted Emmitt as he paused for a moment at the top of the hill.

"Look, Gramps!" Emmitt shouted. "He's waving to me."

It wasn't a friendly wave. Billy was relishing in the fact that he could do something that Emmitt never could. And he wanted Emmitt to know it.

"Don't mind him, E.T. Your brother's being petty and spiteful. This is his way of getting back at you. Don't show that you're upset, else he'll continue to tease you. Remember, forgiveness is the key to peace."

Emmitt's eyes filled with tears. Even though Gramps meant well, such words as *forgiveness* and *peace* couldn't do anything right now to make Emmitt feel better. He so wished he could play outside with the other boys. "I hate it when he makes me feel like a loser. I just want to be able to play with the other boys. And Billy knows it. He's so mean. I would swap anything in the world to sleigh down Death Mountain just once."

Emmitt's Grandfather looked at his grandson with sympathy and concern. In his heart, he would give anything to see Emmitt be able to fulfill his wish.

"That's my dream, Gramps, my wish on my lucky star."

Gramps responded with a far-off look in his eyes. "That was also my dream as a kid – to sleigh down *Death Mountain.*"

"Really? Tell me about it, Gramps. Please."

Gramps closed his eyes. A long silence followed. Emmitt felt that Gramps was trying to bring himself back in time. "I still remember how my heart throbbed and my knees trembled as I climbed up Death Mountain. It seemed the climb up the mountain was as scary as the ride down."

Gramps looked into Emmitt's eyes before he spoke again. "Only the bravest had the courage to fly down *Death Mountain.* That darn mountain gets so icy you can't steer the sleigh away from the big trees at the bottom. A lot of kids got injured because of those trees."

"What about your first ride? Did you get hurt?" Emmitt was so eager to hear about his Gramps' tale that he could barely contain himself.

Gramps smiled with regret. "My first ride was the scariest moment in my life. I lay on my sleigh and looked down the mountain. It was like looking down a sheer cliff. Next thing I know, the wind is howling around me, and the trees at the bottom were rushing up to me like a runaway train. I tried to avoid the trees, but I just couldn't manage it. I crashed right into one 'em and broke my ankle. That first ride was my only ride. I never tried it again. But I never regretted doing it. It was a dream come true. I was so proud I had the courage to do it. Now you know why I walk with a limp."

Gramps paused for a moment and winked at Emmitt. "E.T., keep on wishing on your lucky star because dreams do come true for those who believe. But now I need my rest. There's been enough stress today to last me a lifetime."

"Okay, Gramps. You rest up while I keep an eye on Billy."

*   *   *

Bubba returned to the waiting room at 9:55 and marched directly to Emmitt. Although Emmitt was sleeping, that didn't stop Billy from shaking him awake.

"Wake-up, loser," shouted Billy.

Startled, Emmitt awoke to Billy's violent shaking. He didn't quite know what was going on. He rubbed the sleep from his eyes as best he could. All the while, Billy just stood and watched his brother without care or apology, happily munching on a candy bar and sipping soda out of a can.

"Don't tell me you're going to start crying again," said Billy. "You're such a baby. Are ya going to wake-up grandpa like a little sissy?"

"Buzz off. I can handle myself," replied Emmitt. "I'm not afraid of you, butt-face!" But Emmitt was more nervous than he let on. He just didn't want to show it to his brother.

"Oh, really. Then take this-" Whack! Billy jabbed Emmitt with a nugee to the head while sticking his tongue at him.

"Ouch!" cried out Emmitt. He looked up at his brother, rubbing his head, trying to choke back his tears. He wanted so much to beat up his brother. But he knew he didn't have a chance, not when he was stuck in a wheelchair.

Billy covered his mouth and laughed. He didn't want to laugh too loudly, else he might wake up his grandfather. Then he'd really be in trouble.

As much as Emmitt hated his brother at this moment, he knew now was the time to carry out his grandfather's plan. He took a deep breath and looked straight up at his brother, wiping away his tears. "I know you hate me, Billy. I'd hate me too if I got stuck with a loser brother who couldn't do anything for himself. But I still love you, Billy, because you're my brother. But I didn't ask to be put in this wheelchair. I didn't ask to be sick. I just wish you would love me back. I wish you would make me proud to have a big brother so I can brag to everyone about you. Can't you like me just a little?"

Billy opened his mouth in response, but nothing came out. For once, Billy didn't have a smart aleck response. It was as if the cat got his tongue. Each time he began a response, he would just as quickly close his mouth. Finally, he just shrugged, giving up. Without anything to say, Billy hung his head down and walked away from Emmitt in shame.

Emmitt began to wonder if Gramps' silly plan was about to work. Suddenly, Billy stopped and stood still. Then he turned around and walked back to Emmitt. Standing in front of Emmitt, Billy fixed his eyes on his brother. It was obvious Billy wanted to say something. This time it was something serious.

Billy squatted down next to his brother and whispered in his ear so no one else could hear. "Emmitt, I don't hate you. It's me I hate. I just take everything out on you because you're harmless and I know you can't fight back. I guess that makes me a bully, huh?"

Emmitt couldn't believe what he was hearing. He never thought in a million years Billy could have a soft side. "No, Billy, you're not a bully. Everyone knows you're the strongest in your grade."

Billy smiled. "You're alright, Emmitt, even if you are a runt. But you're my runt. If anyone else calls you that, I'd bop 'em on the head. Just remember, you may be funny-lookin', but you're the smartest little brother in the world. That's your strength. Use it. Don't be a jerk like me. Instead, be a cool Jedi."

58

Emmitt was filled with pride. He couldn't help smiling from ear to ear. "Wow, Billy, thanks for making me feel better. You're the best brother in the world, even if you are a butt-face. But since you're my brother, you are the coolest butt-face."

Billy grinned. "Maybe I should listen to Gramps more often. I really should think before I speak. Is everything cool between us?"

"You betcha! But you really should apologize to Nurse Petersen. That was a mean prank you pulled on her. What were you thinkin', numnuts?"

Billy shrugged and looked down at the floor. "I guess that was a mean thing to do, huh?"

"You really hurt her, Bubba. A big time no-no."

"This is why it doesn't pay to be a jerk. Afterwards, you always have to face up and apologize. I hate apologizing. I mean, especially to Nurse Petersen. She's so scary and mean. It scares me to even look at her. And don't try to tell me it doesn't scare you, either."

"It does," replied Emmitt. "But Bubba, think how people must feel about seeing my face. That's why I feel sorry for Nurse Petersen. The way you treated her is the way people sometimes treat me. It hurts, Billy."

"Yeah, I guess it does." Billy was ashamed of himself. You could see it in his eyes. "Listen, runt, I'm only going to say this once. So you better not laugh. I'm sorry. I'm sorry for teasing you today. I guess I was feeling sorry for myself. It stinks being stuck in this emergency room on Christmas Eve. But I'm sure Dad will find a way to get us out of here tonight and get us home for Christmas. I gotta feeling this day will have a happy ending. Besides, it is Christmas."

Billy found a chair next to Emmitt and spoke louder than Gramp's snoring. "Hey, E.R., I hope the Nutty Professor cures you soon. I heard the police are talkin' about closing down Death Mountain. I'm talking about for good. That means no more sleighing for anyone."

Billy's news alarmed Emmitt. What if he never got his chance to race down the mountain? "Why would they do that?"

"Remember little Troy Syster? You know, the track star?"
"Yeah."

Billy moved closer to Emmitt so he wouldn't have to shout over Gramps snoring. "He just broke his leg tonight on the mountain. Wiped out at the bottom, near the trees. I overheard the police sayin' that they're thinkin' about asking the town to shut the mountain down."

Emmitt was stunned. "That's horrible, Billy. Now I'm never gonna get my chance."

"I'm sorry, little brother." Billy was indeed sympathetic. "But look on the bright side. If they do close it down for good, I'll be known around town as the last kid to ride Death Mountain. Just think, I'll be famous. And so will you. Not bad, huh?"

"Why would I be famous?"

"Because, numnut, you're my brother and it's your fault I was stuck here tonight. Get it?"

"I guess so." Emmitt wasn't too sure, though. "But I would rather ride down Death Mountain than be famous!" Emmitt could only think about what it would be like to race down the most feared mountain in town. "Hey, Billy, tell me about Death Mountain."

Billy's eyes lit up with excitement as he spoke about his ride. "Death Mountain is better than a dream! I must of hit 60 miles an hour. I think the best part is the danger. There's always the chance of getting killed. Just tonight, I barely missed a tree. If I had hit it, I would'a been sitting in a wheelchair just like you. I'll tell ya', though, only the bravest can conquer Death Mountain. You should be lucky to have a brother so brave as me." Billy laughed out loud. He was so proud of himself.

"Would you ride down it again?"

"Are you nuts? I barely survived the first time. I said I was brave, not crazy! There's a reason why they call it Death Mountain, you know."

60

"Like, daaa . . . I'm not stupid, you know. But you mark my words, Billy, I'm gonna ride down that mountain on a sled if it kills me." Emmitt looked Billy in the eyes. Emmitt's face was one of unwavering determination.

"I think you're serious."

Emmitt did not blink. He continued to stare at his brother defiantly.

"Listen, runt, you gotta walk before you run."

"I'm gonna do it, Billy. I'm gonna ride down Death Mountain."

Billy had never seen his little brother so determined. He was almost afraid Emmitt would try to race down Death Mountain by himself, even if it did kill him. "Listen, we'll talk about this later. Let's get some sleep."

Emmitt closed his eyes. Before long, he and Billy dozed in their chairs.

Chapter 23
Feeling-Down-Right
Dumpy-Blue

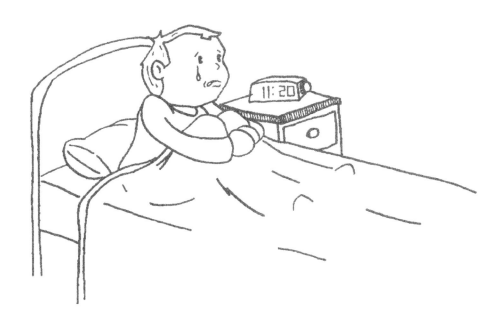

    Nurse Matilda gently shook Gramps to wake him from his nap. The clock read ten fifty. "Wake up, Mr. O'Hara. I wanna move yer and yer sleepin' boys to a room upstairs for the night." She spoke quietly so no one else would hear. "This is no proper place to spend the night."
    Gramps accepted her offer with a smile and a nod. No chair could compete with a bed. Gramps shook Emmitt and Billy awake. Both rubbed the sand from their eyes.

62

Billy raced Emmitt down the empty hallways like a racecar as he followed Gramps and Nurse Matilda to Room 219. When they arrived, the clock in the room read eleven o'clock on the dot. The room was small but clean. It had two beds, two chairs and a window overlooking the hospital entrance. As he looked out the window, Emmitt knew immediately that his job was to stay awake and be the first one to spot the arrival of his parents. The view out the window showed the entrance of the hospital. He knew he wouldn't be able to miss his parents' car.

Gramps and Billy were already asleep when Nurse Matilda dimmed the lights. Before she left, she touched Emmitt's cheek. "I gotta go now. You sure yer gonna be okay?"

"Ms. Maddy, do you have family waiting for you at home tonight?" whispered Emmitt.

"I'm afraid not, child. My family lives in Jamaica. That's a long way from here." Nurse Matilda wondered why Emmitt would ask such a question. "Why do you ask, master Rhodes? Or are yer just bein' nosey?"

Emmitt smiled. "No, I was just wondering why you're movin' aroun' the room so fast? You normally do things at your own pace."

"You noticed, did you? Tell yer the truth, I'm saving most of my money I make here so I can bring my youngest brother, Dwight, to this fine land. I miss him so much, especially now around the holiday time and all. He's kind and gentle like you, boy. I miss the rest of my family too, especially my Moma Francis. I don't feel so lonely for them when I'm with yer family. Can yer understand that, boy?"

"Sure can. But why are you in such a hurry to leave me tonight?"

"That's my business, boy. But since I like yer, I'll tell yer. I'm racin' about here because Nurse Petersen told me I could only have this room for all of yer if I covered the late shift for her tonight. I agreed to her deal being I have no family to rush home to. There, now you know why."

63

Emmitt was struck by Nurse Matilda's sacrifice. He'd never known such generosity outside of his immediate family. Without thinking, he put his arms around her in appreciation. "Thank you, Ms. Maddy, thank you so much for taking care of me like you do."

Nurse Matilda accepted Emmitt's hug with a tearful smile, for she loved Emmitt as if he were her own child. "Master Rhodes, that old lonely girl, Nurse Petersen, is waiting for me downstairs. Now, honey, I'm not one to bust anyone's balloon, yer know, but I don't think that girl's gettin' outta here with all that snow out there."

Emmitt looked outside. He hadn't noticed that the snow was piling up so quickly. In fact, he didn't think anyone would be able to get out of here tonight. There was just too much snow on the ground. He wondered if his parents would even make it to the hospital. After all, if no one could leave, then how could anyone arrive?

"Now, get yer bed sheets up, Master Rhodes. It's time you went to sleep." Nurse Matilda tucked Emmitt into bed. Before leaving, she gave him a kiss on his forehead and a grand smile to which Emmitt gave a unique smile of his own.

*   *   *

Everybody was sleeping peacefully in Room 219 at eleven twenty. That is, everybody except Emmitt. He was too upset to sleep. He couldn't figure out why his mother kept telling him that he was born under a lucky star. If he was so special, then why couldn't he walk and talk like everybody else. Emmitt just felt down right dumpy blue.

In hopes of changing his crummy mood, Emmitt decided to re-read his Christmas letter to Santa.

64

Chapter 24
A Letter to Santa

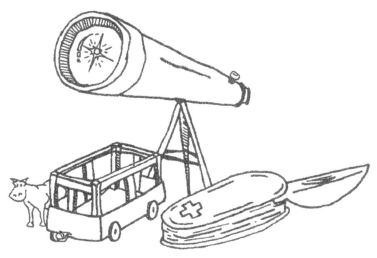

The letter was simple:

Dear Santa,
   Hope you're feeling Ho-Ho happy.
   Stay toasty warm and shine up Rudolph's red nose so bright.
   Here's my Christmas wish list.
   #1 – I'd love to have a Swiss Army pocketknife, the one with a compass.
   #2 - A cattle car for my Lionel train set.
   #3 - A telescope to look at my lucky star up close.

   Merry Christmas!

                    Love,
                    E.T.

65

Just as Emmitt finished reading his Christmas letter to Santa, his eyes started to shut. Sleep finally came to him and he slept. Not even Gramp's snoring could keep Emmitt awake.

Emmitt slept for many minutes. Suddenly, he woke up and opened his eyes. Maybe it was one of Gramp's more powerful snorts or maybe it was something else entirely. Whatever it was, Emmitt woke in time to see the clock, which read eleven forty five.

Emmitt rubbed his eyes as he sat up in bed and looked at the window behind Gramps' chair. The roads were covered with a thick layer of ice and slush, and the blanket of snow falling from the sky was blown by a strong wind, creating towering snowdrifts. Emmitt realized that only Santa's magical sleigh was equipped to travel in this Christmas wonderland of snow, ice and wind.

This saddened Emmitt. For the likelihood of Mom's car miraculously turning into the hospital entrance before daybreak was dwindling by the minute. But he refused to allow his spirits to sink. There was always hope but his present problem was staying awake. It was late and not even Gramps' lion-roaring snoring could keep him awake. Only one thing could prevent his eyes from closing- solving the riddle to the three mysterious stories Gramps had told earlier in the day.

Emmitt especially enjoyed thinking about these puzzling stories because they were a lot like his own life – hard to figure.

Chapter 25
Hope for a Better Tomorrow

Emmitt leaned back into his curled-up pillow as he began to think about Gramps' three Christmas stories. He smiled as he remembered how J.C. Pepperweather played on his lap as Gramps began telling his first story in the den of his house.

Gramps' pocketful of magical stories all began with a question.

"E.T., do you think the three Wise Men figured out the importance and purpose of the Child born under a lucky star that first Christmas night?" As Gramps asked, he slowly moved back and forth in his rocking chair. He smiled as he examined Emmitt's question mark face. Realizing Emmitt did not have an answer yet, he continued.

"Once upon a time, there were three Royal Wise Men who studied the stars in search of answers to their questions and dreams. One particular star, which we now know as the Christmas Star, led these three Kings on a journey that ended at a stable in Bethlehem. And in this stable a special child was born."

Gramps' eyes gleamed as he told his story.

"This child, this Royal Child, had power to move the very stars in the heavens," Gramps continued. "Yet he was born in poverty and hunger. These three Royal Wise Men, however, brought the Child presents in honor of the Child's mysterious power over heaven and earth."

Gramps abruptly stopped rocking in his chair, raised his eyebrows and leaned forward to ask Emmitt another question. "Do you think the three Wise Men understood the significance of Christmas or do you think they merely gave presents without thinking, like most people do today?"

Emmitt took a few seconds to gather his thoughts before responding. "It seems the three Wise Men were more interested in learning about the science of stars than worshipping the birth of the King of the heavens."

Gramps was impressed. But he wanted to see if Emmitt really understood. "Why do you say that, Emmitt?"

Emmitt took his time answering. He didn't want to disappoint his grandfather. "The three Kings left the Child after they gave him "presents" but before knowing what His *presence* on Earth meant. It seems that the three Wise Men gave gifts to the Child without realizing the gift the Child was trying to offer them."

Gramps was indeed impressed with his grandson, which could be seen in his sparkling eyes. "That's a mighty fine answer, Emmitt. But what was the gift the Child was trying to offer to the three Wise Men?"

Emmitt shut his eyes for a few seconds to gather his thoughts before he responded. "Gramps, I'm not really sure. I need some help."

Gramps sat back in his rocker, lit his pipe and started blowing smoke circles in the air from his mouth before replying. "E.T., you do realize you're asking me to explain the meaning of Christmas?"

Emmitt nodded with his head. "I guess so, Gramps."

68

"The kings of this world have always ruled over their subjects. The Child of the stable had awesome powers, but unlike the kings of history, He came to serve, not to rule," Gramps responded. "This Child called Jesus taught the world how to serve and care for the poor, the unwanted, and the sick. To be His follower, you simply have to follow His example. Words are not enough. Action is required. It is easy to say you forgive. But it is much harder to hug the person who just slapped your face."

Gramps stopped speaking for a moment to look into Emmitt's eyes. "Now, listen up, son! This Child's nobility was hidden somewhere in His weakness, somewhere in His loneliness and also somewhere in His humility. Jesus entered the world to offer the lonely souls, the unwanted oddballs, the uninvited outcasts and all the E.T.'s of this world hope for a better tomorrow."

"Gramps," Emmitt interrupted. "I do have hope that tomorrow will be better than today, but I still feel like an error. I wasn't born like everyone else. Why did God have to make me so ugly and disabled? I just wanna be like everyone else."

Gramps chewed on his pipe. He looked at his grandson and shook his finger back and forth. "You're smarter than that, Emmitt. If you were an error that would mean God is less than perfect. And God is anything but imperfect. He is a master craftsman and he doesn't make errors. You know that. Never doubt your importance, my boy. There is a reason for everything. You have to have faith. And faith is believing in things when common sense tells you not to."

"But Gramps, I need an answer. I don't wanna go through the rest of my life wondering why I'm such a freak. It hurts to be me." Emmitt eyes began to water.

"E.T., that's unfair! I don't have the answers you seek. You know darn well that only God knows our purpose in life. You have to trust Him. And in fairness, look at the gifts you have. You have a family who loves you and would do anything for you. You know how many "normal" people there are in the world who would trade places with you just to have a mom and dad who hugs them and kisses them? Let me explain somethin' to you, young man. Delivering Billy took a lot out of your mom. Nearly killed her, I tell you. Dr. Clarence told her another pregnancy -- she could lose both herself and the baby. Nearly broke her heart hearing this. She just wanted one more baby. Just one. And boy did she pray for it. I swear I know there's a God up there because suddenly Dr. Clarence called and told us he had a baby for us.'

"I remember that day like it was yesterday. I rushed your mother to Dr. Clarence's office in a heartbeat. Before we could even say hello, he told us a baby boy had been left on the steps of the hospital. No note, no explanation -- just the most adorable baby boy in a basket. That was enough for your mother. She said, 'That's my little boy. That's my Emmitt Thomas Rhodes. I knew God would answer my prayers.'

"That's when Dr. Clarence's face drooped with sadness. He told us that you were disabled from the waist down, and what an emotional and financial burden you would be. They should think it over. That's as far as he got. Nothing and no one was going to talk your mother out of keeping you. As far as she was concerned, you were her little angel sent from heaven on Christmas morning. We've celebrated your birthday on Christmas ever since."

"Gramps," asked Emmitt with a little apprehension, "have I been a burden to the family?"

Gramps stared at Emmitt with intense eyes and a firm jaw. "Your mother is convinced that you're a Christmas present sent from heaven. I judge a person's worth by his capacity to love others without reserve. After ten years of knowing you, you've given me and this family enough blankets of love to warm the coldest hearts in the coldest places on earth. And there's still a lot more blankets in your endless heart."

Gramps' words sobered Emmitt. He realized that he was real lucky to have such a great family. He could only imagine how bad it would be if he had to go through life with no one to take care of him.

Gramps puffed on his pipe as he watched Emmitt digest his words. He was proud that his grandson wouldn't give in to pity. After a few seconds, Gramps got out of his chair, walked over to Emmitt and gave him a bear hug. "Maybe it's only when we're in paradise that we'll be able to know the deepest *whys* of our life. But in the meantime, remember this: *you bring an importance to my existence. And don't you ever forget that!"*

Emmitt hugged his grandfather with the deepest affection. He felt ashamed that he ever doubted God's kindness and perfection.

Chapter 26
Simple Words With
A Powerful Meaning

Gramps' second story began with a riddle. "Which is stronger, rock or iron?"

"What kind of question is that, Gramps. Everyone knows iron is stronger."

Gramps smiled and asked another question. "Have you ever heard the story of David and Goliath?"

This time Emmitt shook his head up and down. "Sure, I know the story. It's one of my favorites. It's about a boy who fights a giant with a . . . rock." Emmitt suddenly realized the point his Gramps was trying to make. "Wow, Gramps. Maybe iron isn't stronger."

"But what's stronger than rock and iron?" asked Gramps.

This time Emmitt knew the answer. "God."

"Why do you say that?"

"Because David would never have beaten Goliath without help. He knew he couldn't win the battle with only his strength. So he asked for God's help and God gave it to him. And boy did he ever!"

"And you, Emmitt, are my David. You may not have much strength, but what you have is God. With Him on your side, you can beat all the Goliaths of the world."

Gramps took a deep breath before he continued. "Imitate David's faith and let go all of your fears to God. God's power can strength your weakness when you pray for help."

Emmitt smiled and thought about all the adventures he could have with God by his side guiding and helping him.

Chapter 27
The Lesson of
The Stable

Gramps' third story began with another question. "Why did God pick a smelly, dirty old stable for the birth of His one and only Son?"

Emmitt wasn't sure of the answer, but tried to answer it anyway. "Maybe God was trying to teach people a lesson without using words."

"That's a good answer, E.T. A very good answer. But what do you think the lesson is?"

Emmitt thought long and hard before answering. "Don't complain or say things are unfair?"

Gramps paused for a moment to puff on his pipe before he spoke. "Exactly. In other words, not even the king of kings was born in royalty. For a true king is royal in heart and mind, not in the house he lives in or in the number of basketballs he can dunk or the amount of money he has."

Emmitt blushed with pride. He liked receiving compliments.

74

"So if the Son of God never complained about growing up poor and dying on a cross, don't you think it's unfair of you to complain about being in a wheelchair?"

Emmitt squirmed in his chair. He was embarrassed by his grandfather's question. He also knew his grandfather was right. "Gosh, Gramps, since you put it that way, I guess I have been feeling sorry for myself. How do know me so good?"

Gramps smiled. "Because I have also felt sorry for myself. But when I think of the sacrifice Jesus made for us, I realize that I should be the happiest person alive. With God's embrace and love, anything is possible. And if Jesus never complained about his life, then who are we to complain about ours."

Emmitt knew his Gramps was right. From that moment on, he secretly vowed he would never feel sorry for himself again.

"Now, my boy, do you want to hear a secret saying my grandfather once told me a long time ago?"

Emmitt nodded.

"Whenever you question why bad things happen to you, ask yourself one more question. Why did bad things happen to Jesus? If you can answer the second question, then you should be able to answer the first one."

Gramps ended this story with one final remark. "The lesson of the stable is simple. To share like He shared, to give like He gave, to serve like He served."

Emmitt had a lot to think about. But he was feeling a lot better than he had. Just thinking about Jesus made him want to be a better person.

E.T.'s eyes were closed but he was seeing perfectly clear.

Chapter 28
A Wish on A Star

Having thought about Gramps' three Christmas stories, Emmitt no longer felt tired. Emmitt's mind was busy, as it raced from one thought to the next, not allowing sleep to creep in. He realized that this was a pretty good day after all. He escaped a car accident coming to the hospital, he received good news from the Nutty Professor that his health wasn't in danger, and best of all, he received a first ever apology from Billy the Brat.

It occurred to Emmitt that sometimes-good things are hidden even in the worse of situations. We just need to find them. He hated coming to the hospital. But when he did, he always got a chance to see Spanky, his best friend in the whole world.

Good fortune was something to wish for and he did.

And there was one more wish Emmitt wanted to add to his Christmas wish list. He knew it was the type of wish neither Santa nor his parents could get him. And he also knew that to ask for another wish could deprive someone else of his or her wish. Was that selfish?

He relaxed himself and words seemed to shout from his inner voice, 'if you ask for too much, numnut, then someone else will get too little! Don't you get it: that's opposite from the sharing values taught in the Christmas story.'

Emmitt responded resentfully to his inner voice of reason, 'I deserve one more gift than normal kids because I was born with so much less. I'm not wishing for more than I need. I need something more than I have. I do get it, numnut! For one time in my misfit life I want to feel like I belong in this world.'

Emmitt hastily closed his eyes and hoped beyond sensible hope that his wish would be heard and granted as a sort of birthday gift. 'I'm special! I was born under a lucky star like the Child of the stable.' He sat up in bed and looked at the ceiling as he prayed.

What he wanted more than anything else in the whole wide world was a pair of strong healthy legs so he could walk away from the misery of the wheelchair and climb Death Mountain like a true adventurer and hero.

Emmitt wished that this miracle would be granted to him on Christmas morning, his birthday.

Chapter 29
Reality Of Imagination

    Emmitt had always believed in miracles. He believed his imagination had a cosmic energy force to change reality. He believed that every person on earth and every being throughout the universe had the power to command unusual happenings to happen. With true belief and unbending faith, he had always felt that anything was possible.

    He believed that snowmen could dance, that bunnies hide Easter eggs and Tooth Fairies sprinkled sleeping dust on children while they exchanged their teeth for money.

    He believed that a wish on a Shining Star could make the impossible so very possible. Emmitt's belief in miracles grew stronger after he read a book called <u>Born Under A Lucky Star</u>.

The book described a miracle as nothing more than an unusual happening that shocks someone because it's unexpected. It affirmed his gut feeling that most people label unusual happenings as miracles because they see only what they expect to see and simply miss and overlook the number of miracles that flow naturally in the normal events of each and every day.

Grandma Katherine and Emmitt always spoke about how a wish on a lucky Star could come true. In fact, the book was the last thing Grandma Katherine spoke to Emmitt about before she died. Emmitt tried to recall her last words to him but he couldn't. Sleep was overcoming him again. This time, he couldn't fight it.

Just when he thought he would fall asleep, a strange thing happened that kept him fully awake for a good minute. It seemed Grandma Katherine's soothing voice whispered in his ear as if she was bending down to kiss him goodnight. *Listen up my little bookworm, miracles are granted only to people who see life through the eyes of God's reality. If you want your wish to be granted tonight you must believe, without any doubt.*

With those whispered words, Emmitt fell asleep. He dreamt that his prayers were answered. In his dream, he asked, "Please, God, grant me my wish. Let me climb Death Mountain just once. Let me feel your wind as I race down that mountain as no one has ever done."

*   *   *

Emmitt dreamed of seeing his Star.

The Star was ready to shine on him tonight.

Part V
A Christmas Adventure

Chapter 30
A Wake-up Call
From Above

    Emmitt's eyes shot open from a dead sleep. He didn't know why. He checked the time on his pocket watch. Exactly midnight. It was Christmas and no one was stirring, not even Bubba Billy.
    The room was dark, except for a narrow beam of light that penetrated the window. The light appeared to radiate from the very heavens, brightening the darkness in the room.
    And it was this light that made Emmitt aware that the snow had stopped falling. He also noticed that Gramps' rhythmic snoring had also stopped, which gave Emmitt the impression that time itself had stopped. Only the soft tapping of the wind against the windowpane intruded upon the quiet of the room.
    A sense of peace and comfort washed over Emmitt. He was at ease. If this was a dream, Emmitt thought, he wasn't ready to wake up.

Chapter 31
A Bang On
The Door

Suddenly, the door slammed open with a mighty earsplitting bang, as if a mighty hurricane gust had attacked it. Emmitt couldn't believe that the door didn't fly off its hinges. More surprising was that Gramps and Billy didn't wake up.

In a blink of any eye, a small figure appeared in the darkened doorway. Emmitt couldn't believe what he saw. His face lit up with an ear-to-ear smile. "Hans Orion!" shouted Emmitt. "Gosh, what are you doin' here? I never thought I'd meet you!"

Hans spoke without speaking. He was able to talk to Emmitt with his thoughts alone. And he did so with a huge smile. "Your wish on a Star has been heard," replied Hans. "Are you ready for some fun, young Emmitt? Tonight, your every wish is my command."

82

"Awesome! You really mean it?"

"Would I be here if I weren't?"

"Wow, Mr. Orion, I don't know what to say."

"You can start by calling me Hans, young man. The Orion stuck because that's the planet I come from."

"You betcha, Hans. And your wish is my command too!" Emmitt was so giggly happy that he could barely contain himself.

Hans, too, was gleeful. Excitement seemed to radiate from his very eyes, brightening the entire room. In fact, the energy radiating out of Han's eyes activated all the electrical gadgets in the room, one by one. As much ringing and clanging and buzzing and whistles rattling as there was, surprisingly none of it disturbed Gramps or Billy. They continued to sleep as peacefully as ever.

"Sorry, young Emmitt, my excitement does that. I seemed to have *over-energized* the room."

Emmitt couldn't stop laughing. It seemed too perfect having Hans Orion in the very same room as him.

With a twitch of Hans' nose the room became still again. That's all it took. Such was the power of Hans. "My child-like excitement has gotten the best of me again. That's better, I should think."

Emmitt sat up in his bed with his head cupped restfully between his hands. "Welcome, Hans. It's so very nice to meet ya!"

Chapter 32
The First Step To Freedom, The Sight of Light

    Hans suddenly leapt into the room like a drunken acrobat, stumbling and falling, leaping his way toward Gramps. It appeared Hans was trying to fly with every leap. Each time he came down, he would fall to the ground in a heap. Then he would try to stand on his feet, which turned into a balancing act. At that moment, Hans reminded Emmitt of the Strawman in the <u>Wizard of OZ</u>.

    Hans greeted Gramps by gently caressing his brow with both his hands. Suddenly, Gramp's face began to glow and transform. Then Grandma Katherine's *happy smile* miraculously appeared on his face. Emmitt couldn't believe his eyes, but at that moment he didn't think he could be any happier.

    Hans slowly moved away from Gramps. Then he jumped like a kangaroo to the window that overlooked the hospital entrance. At the window, Hans knelt on one knee and pointed to the sky, while he wiggled his finger for Emmitt to join him. He wanted Emmitt to worship the sight of the brilliant light above.

Chapter 33
An Unmistakable Grin

The unmistakable grin on Hans' jolly face told Emmitt that something special was about to happen. Hans continued to speak to Emmitt without words. Emmitt could hear everything in Hans' mind.

"Young Emmitt, I have come to answer your prayers," Hans spoke. "Sit back and enjoy the ride. Anything you can imagine, we can do."

"Just tell me what to do, Hans!" Emmitt was so happy he could have jumped up and down on his bed.

"Do you trust me, Emmitt?"

" Of course I do, Hans."

"Then you must do everything I tell you to do."

"Anything you say."

"For starters, I can't guarantee you that your wish is going to come true. A lot depends on you."

"But, Hans, this isn't your first time helping someone with a wish, is it?"

"First time?" Hans couldn't believe his ears. "Young man, I've been doing this a long time. In fact, I'm the one who helped David defeat Goliath." Hans chuckled at Emmitt's doubting. "I'm Hans Orion, Emmitt. I only get the most important jobs. You, my boy, are right now the most important person in the whole universe, as far as I'm concerned." Hans' eyes sparkled with laughter.

"Wow, Hans, am I that important?" asked Emmitt.

"You sure are, young man. But just remember, in the Lord's eyes, everyone is important. Now, any questions before we start?"

"Just one. It's about David."

"Well, you're asking the right person. I know a lot about David."

"How did David find the courage to fight a giant twice his size?"

Hans grinned as he scratched his chin. "Before I answer that, first let me tell you something about your hero. David was the youngest boy in a family of soldiers. While his older brothers were nobly fighting in the King's army, he was biting his nails in boredom, tending his fathers sheep herd. Because of this, David didn't have many friends. He grew up very lonely and sad. The only friends he made were the lost sheep he rescued. Did you know that, Emmitt?"

"I never heard that part of the story. Tell me more, Hans."

"David became a bitter and unhappy young man because he hated being an unimportant shepherd. He craved for the fame and excitement of a soldier's life."

"Then how did David become a hero?"

Hans' eyes sparked and his ears wiggled as he spoke about David. Emmitt laughed each time this happened. Hans looked so goofy wiggling his ears. "David prayed each and every dawn. He sang to the heavens for an answer to his prayers. The Lord could no longer ignore him and sent me to help him with his wish."

"Then who killed Goliath? You or David?" asked Emmitt.

86

"David was a very strong-minded young man, very much like you, young Emmitt. David found strength in the power of God's presence with my help. He learned how to conquer his fear with prayer. I found five stones for David's sling that day, but it was David alone who walked out on that battlefield and slew Goliath. Do you have the courage to do the same?"

"You betcha, Hans." Emmitt truly felt that he could do anything on this most special night of the year.

"Then walk to me, young Emmitt. Come see the Christmas Star that shines for you, above all."

Hans' words energized Emmitt. Emmitt took many long, deep breaths. Then in a pure act of faith he propped himself up, with just the strength of his hands, and flung himself off the side of the bed.

Emmitt soared into the air. But instead of crashing to the floor, he miraculously landed on his own two feet as if he'd been using them all his life. Emmitt couldn't believe his eyes. There he was, standing on his very own, his own feet supporting his body weight for the first time in his life. Emmitt was delirious with happiness. He couldn't believe he was standing on two legs.

Emmitt looked up in amazement, and without hesitation, leaped on his bed. He jumped up and down on his bed as if he'd never been on one before. He laughed and giggled, clapping his hands, and flinging his arms about like a wild chicken. After he had his fill of jumping up and down, he leaped off the bed, walked passed Gramps and Bubba, and ran to Hans, who was grinning as much as Emmitt.

Hans caught Emmitt in his outstretched arms and gave him a mighty bear hug.

"Oh, Hans, thank you so much. I can finally walk like everyone else," said Emmitt.

"You're so welcome, young man. And this is just the beginning. Now, kneel with me so we can see the Star that granted you your wish."

Emmitt knelt next to Hans at the window and looked at the light beaming from the sky. Awesome rainbow colors shone magnificently from Emmitt's Christmas Star. Emmitt couldn't find the words to describe the beauty he was seeing.

"In His presence, Emmitt, everyone is perfect. Be happy and enjoy the Lord's gifts. Merry Christmas and Happy Birthday! Your wish has been granted, you lucky Emmitt." said Hans.

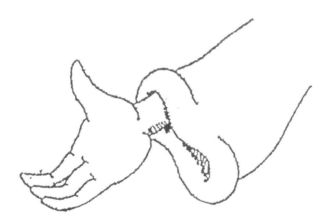

Chapter 34
Silent Night
Holy Night

Hans left Emmitt at the window and stumbled his way back to the door. Before he left, he pulled his miniature snow boots off his feet and tossed them to Emmitt. "Use these for your journey up Death Mountain, young Emmitt. Ho-Ho-Ho and a very Merry Christmas to you."

Then Hans left with a jovial grin as suddenly as he had come.

Emmitt quickly dressed for his winter adventure. He couldn't wait to get started. Gramps and Billy were still asleep. Nothing had stirred them, not Hans or their gleeful shouting. Emmitt rushed out of the room in search of Hans with Hans' boots tightly tied to his feet.

The hallway was empty and soundless. Emmitt couldn't help but wonder if this wasn't a dream. Just to make sure, he pinched his arm. "Ouch!" The pain answered Emmitt's worries. This was no dream, after all. Still, he couldn't believe this was happening. He couldn't believe that he was walking and running. Most especially, he couldn't believe he was about to climb up Death Mountain.

Before running out the room, he stopped abruptly and looked up in the air and began to plead again in prayer. "Please, Lord, please grant me one more wish. I promise I won't wish for anything else. Never, ever, ever! Please let Spanky be at the hospital. Please let her join me."

Chapter 35
Listed Dead
Or Alive

    Emmitt raced out the room. He suddenly stopped at the nurse's station. It was deserted. He crossed his fingers and closed both his eyes. He was scared to look at the inpatient blackboard. He slowly opened one of his eyes to peek at the board.
    Emmitt jumped up in joy, fists pumping in the air, when he saw Lacey-Anne Ashley was listed. Spanky was in Room 245.
The room was only a few doors down. It took him only five hops, two skips and a jump to get there.

Without knocking, Emmitt opened Spanky's door and ran inside. He stopped when he noticed Hans stumbling his way around the room towards Spanky, who was sound asleep in her bed.

Spanky's parents were sleeping in chairs on each side of the bed. Spanky and her parents were unaware of the brilliant glow coming from Hans' eyes that bathed the room in white splintering brilliance.

Emmitt watched Hans gently caress Spanky's forehead. He began to softly rub his thumbs in a slow, circular motion over her eyes. It appeared to Emmitt that Hans was trying to massage the terrible pain of her sickness out of Spanky's memory.

Then Hans snapped his fingers, and Spanky's eyes bolted open. She never looked more beautiful to Emmitt. Before he could say a word, Spanky leapt out of her bed, ran to the door and hugged Emmitt with all her might.

Chapter 36
Touched By
A Smile

After a long hug, Spanky released Emmitt and stepped back. She couldn't believe it. Emmitt was standing on his own two feet. "Oh, E.T., I'm so happy for you. You can finally walk. Is it everything you thought it would be?"

Emmitt was too excited to talk. All he could do was give Spanky his two thumbs up.

" E.T., who's the little man with the glowing eyes. Was it him who taught you to walk?"

"Nope. That's Hans Orion. He's my Starman. And he didn't teach me to walk. He showed me. He showed me that anything is possible just by putting my faith in the Lord. If I can imagine it, it can come true."

"Wow!" said Spanky. "Can he show me, too? I mean, can he show me how to get better?"

"You're already there, knucklehead," Emmitt giggled.

Spanky realized that it was true. She felt better than she had in a long time, as if she had been reborn. She squeezed Emmitt's hand in excitement. "E.T., look at Hans, he's disappearing!"

Hans vanished from sight with a twitch of his nose and a snap of his finger. He left them with a smile, his ears waving goodbye.

"That was so cool," Spanky said. She stood motionless in a state of shock. With each passing second she felt healthier and healthier, as if she'd never been sick in her life. "You're right, E.T., we're somewhere beyond the rainbow. I feel so wonderful here, like there's no pain anywhere in my body. I've never felt so healthy and alive. Hey, let's go outside and play in the snow. What do you say?"

Emmitt smiled from ear to ear. That's exactly what he wanted to do.

Spanky dressed quickly for her Christmas adventure and was ready in a flash. Just as she was about to leave, Spanky turned to her parents. She couldn't believe they were still sleeping in their chairs. They were completely unaware of what was happening in the room.

Spanky couldn't leave without raining on them enough hugs and kisses to last them a lifetime.

Spanky stepped away from her parents and was about to follow Emmitt out the door when some mysterious force stopped her. She turned away from Emmitt and looked back at her parents. Something told her this would be the last time she would see them. A voice inside her told her she would not be returning. Warm tears began to roll down her cheeks. She loved her parents so much, she couldn't imagine a life without them. But she also knew they could hear her thoughts and that they would understand.

"I'm going to miss you, Mommy and Daddy. Thank you so much for loving me and taking care of me. I love you guys so much in return. I have to go now because I've been invited to Emmitt's birthday party. Remember that I'm not alone. I'm in good hands."

Spanky looked back towards the door and spotted Emmitt waving impatiently for her to join him in the hallway. She knew it was time to leave her parents and find the little man with the bright radiant eyes. She was ready to begin her Christmas adventure.

Spanky ran out of the room without looking back. She grabbed Emmitt's hand securely in hers and marched down the hallway in search of Hans, laughing and giggling all the way.

Chapter 37
A Need for Presence...
Not Presents

Emmitt and Spanky knew Hans would be outside waiting for them. So, dressed and ready for a winter adventure, they ran to the exit door, hearts pounding in their chest with anticipation.

They opened the exit door and entered a different world. Things were not the same. They were greeted by snowballs falling from the sky, and snowmen dancing in the snow. This must be a fairyland, they thought. But whose?

They looked up at the large clock in the hospital steeple. Midnight. It was still midnight. Time had stopped!

But not the Christmas Star. It still shone brightly in the sky, shooting beams of light on Emmitt and Spanky, giving them warmth and comfort on this wintry night.

Chapter 38
Whistling A Happy Tune . . .
A Heavenly Sound

    Emmitt heard Gramps' familiar whistle in the mild breeze. He stood still to listen to its peaceful melody when WHACK! A snowball hit him in the back of the head. He looked behind him and saw Spanky with a devilish grin on her face.

    Before he could react, Spanky ran and tackled Emmitt to the snowy ground. All the animals of the nearby woods joined in: flying squirrels, nutty chipmunks, singing birds, talking rabbits, a red nose reindeer and even a smelly skunk.

    They played for hours in the snow, never tiring. Not even the cold stopped their merriment. In this wonderland, snow never melted and never made anyone cold.

Each time Emmitt and Spanky looked at the steeple clock, it continued to read twelve o'clock. Time really had stopped for them.

And Emmitt's Christmas star continued to shine, adding more magic to this most heavenly night.

Emmitt stopped suddenly to look for Hans. He spotted him at the foot of Death Mountain, standing still with a broad grin on his face. Hans stood barefoot in the snow, dressed only in his shepherd's outfit. He, too, was unaffected by the cold. Looking at him, Emmitt knew that this magicland belonged to Hans.

What attracted Emmitt's attention most of all was what Hans was holding in his right hand. Hans held the biggest and sleekest sleigh he had ever seen. Emmitt realized he and Spanky could both fit on it. Could that be for them?

Chapter 39
Climbing the Mountain
Called Death

Hans waved to Emmitt and Spanky to come over. "Come on, you two."

They rushed to Hans.

"Is that for us, Hans?" asked Emmitt and Spanky together.

"Yessiree. Just for the two of you."

Emmitt and Spanky were too joyous to respond. They just looked at the sleigh. They had never seen anything like it. They could probably go a hundred miles an hour on it.

"Well, what are you waiting for?" asked Hans. "Up you go. You got a long climb ahead of you."

Emmitt and Spanky couldn't wait another second. Now was the moment of truth. Now was the time to conquer their fear and fulfill their dreams. They began their climb up Death Mountain.

It took every ounce of their energy to climb the most feared mountain in town. They slipped, they slid, they fell, but they trudged on, helped by the other. If one fell, the other lent a hand. If one got scared, the other offered words of encouragement. But without struggle, both knew they would never appreciate the thrill to follow.

They at last made it to the top of Death Mountain. They huffed and they puffed, but here they were, on top of the Mountain of Death. They stood on the highest point of the mountain. They could see all of Bethlehem for miles. At that moment, Emmitt and Spanky were the lords of all creation – or that's how they felt. It seemed the world existed only for them. Neither had ever been so high up in the air in their lives.

"Boy, E.T., Death Mountain seems so much higher standing on it than looking up at it," said Spanky.

"Tell me about it. We must be on top of the world."

"Well, what are we waiting for? Let's do it."

"You betcha."

Emmitt sat in the front of the sleigh and Spanky sat right behind him. They both looked down the mountain. It looked like a sheer cliff.

"Hold on, Spanky!" screamed Emmitt.

Emmitt gave a little shove. In a flash, they were racing down the mountain. One minute they were sitting still. The next minute they were speeding down the mountain at fifty miles and hour, and gaining even more speed by the second.

Chapter 40
With A Crash . . .
It Was Over

    Down they went. Emmitt was in charge of steering. Spanky was in charge of screaming with joy. In no time, both were screaming in delight. They zipped down the Mountain of Death like a runaway train. They reached a hundred miles as Emmitt had *imagined*. Their hearts pounded a thousand beats a minute. Their lungs yelled loud enough to be heard around the world.

    And then something strange happened. Emmitt caught a glimpse of the hospital clock. It no longer read twelve o'clock. It had moved to one past twelve. Time had started up again. Then he caught a glimpse of Hans petting a deer and heard him speak to him without words. "It's time for me to move on, young Emmitt."

Emmitt suddenly felt Spanky's gentle grip slide off his back. Then she flew out of the sleigh, reaching for her star in the sky. Spanky waved goodbye to Emmitt from the sky, giving him a radiant smile.

She rose higher and higher, like a shooting star, then spoke to Emmitt like Hans did, without words. "See ya, my friend. It's time for me to move on, too. Happy birthday and merry Christmas. Love you."

Hans joined Spanky in the sky. He leaped up and was soon flying with her, both going up higher and higher like two birds in flight. Then Emmitt lost his concentration. He couldn't steer properly, especially at a hundred miles and hour. BANG! Emmitt crashed into a large oak tree at full speed. As quickly as it had begun, the ride was over.

Part VI
A Temporary Stop Over
Stuck In a Holding Pattern

Chapter 41
The Accident

    Emmitt couldn't open his eyes, but he was awake. He guessed he was in the hospital by the mattress he was lying on and the voices around him. The first voice he heard was the Nutty Professor's. "Mr. and Mrs. Rhodes, I wish there were an easy way of saying this, but I'm afraid there isn't. Your son suffered a life-threatening blow to the head. Odds of a recovery from this type of injury are low. He's in a coma. There's no telling how long he could be like this. It's now a waiting game. I'm afraid his fate is in the hands of God."

    Emmitt's parents took the news with pain and sadness. Both were too numb to respond. All they could do was cuddle in each other's arms as Doctor Clarence left the room.

Captain Rhodes whispered in his wife's ear. "How could this happen? There's no way Emmitt could have done this on his own. Someone had to have played a part in the accident. But who?"

The same questions ran through Annie's head. She spoke softly to her husband, holding back her tears as best she could. "We should ask Nurse Petersen. She's the one who found Emmitt in the snow."

Mr. and Mrs. Rhodes left the room, leaving Emmitt by himself. But Emmitt didn't feel alone. He heard a soothing whistle, which could only come from Gramps. Good 'ol Gramps. He's always there when Emmitt needed him the most.

The coma didn't hurt Emmitt. Being away from his Dad did. To Emmitt, being in a coma felt like he landed in a place where bodily movement wasn't important or needed. It was a place of darkness and shadows, a place to think and reflect on the past.

Emmitt thought about J.C. Pepperweather and his friends, Spanky and Hans. Emmitt also wondered if his mother - the dream chaser herself - would be able to see beyond the obvious. He was afraid his mom wouldn't be able to see that this was a test of her faith.

Emmitt said a prayer for his Mom, asking God to help her find strength in her time of need.

Chapter 42
Billy Gets the Blame

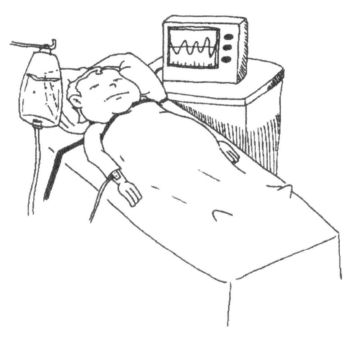

    Emmitt's parents didn't have to search hard or long to find Nurse Petersen. She was sleeping, slouched in a chair at the nursing station. Nurse Petersen was wiggling to find a comfortable position in her uncomfortable chair when Annie O'Hara startled her by shaking her shoulder. "Nurse Petersen, please wake up. I must talk to you about my son."

    Nurse Petersen awoke immediately, even though she was groggy from her nap. "What was that?"

    "What happened to Emmitt, Nurse Petersen? What happened to my son?" asked Annie.

107

Nurse Petersen was now fully awake. "Well, let's see, now. I was stuck here last night because of the storm, like everyone else. I couldn't get to sleep, so I decided to go outside to brush the snow off my car. As I was walking to my car, I spotted a little boy at the base of Death Mountain. The little boy turned out to be Emmitt with snow boots tied to his feet. I mean, I just couldn't believe it was Emmitt of all people."

"Do you know how my son got there?" interrupted Captain Rhodes. "You do realize that Emmitt can't walk?"

"I don't know, Captain Rhodes. Really, I don't. But I have a hunch your son, Billy, might."

"Why would you say that?" questioned Captain Rhodes.

Nurse Petersen smiled with regret. "With all due respect, Captain Rhodes, Billy's a prankster. He embarrassed me in front of everybody in the waiting room yesterday by saying I should ride a broom to Oz. Everyone laughed at me except for E.T. and Mr. O'Hara. Captain Rhodes, that boy needs a good spanking! He's turning into a real brat!"

"Sweetheart, she's right," said Annie. "It makes sense. We all know what a terrible prankster Billy can be. He could easily have tricked Emmitt into going for a sleigh ride down Death Mountain. And he's foolish and strong enough to carry Emmitt without a wheelchair. It all adds up, if you think about it."

Annie turned to Nurse Petersen and embraced her. "Thank you for caring for my Emmitt. And I'm so sorry Billy hurt your feelings. I promise we'll punish Billy for his behavior."

Tears started rolling down Nurse Petersen's face as she hugged Annie back. For the first time in many years Nurse Petersen felt compassion for another person. She held on to the hug for a long time, while Annie cried in her arms.

Nurse Petersen realized at that moment that the greatest thing in life is to be loved. If only someone would love her.

Chapter 43
Having A Miserable Week

Many things happened the week following Emmitt's accident. Being in a coma wasn't the only tragedy to strike the Rhodes family. Emmitt heard through snippets of conversation from the nurses that his friend, Spanky, had died in her bed. Worst of all, so did his Gramps.

Emmitt didn't know who he would miss more. He loved Spanky because she was the one true friend who understood him. She accepted him as a friend even with his handicap and his funny face. She never made fun of him or teased him like the other kids.

Then there was his Gramps. What would Emmitt's life have been without Gramps. He was a father, a friend, and a guardian angel wrapped up in one. Emmitt thought about the thousands of little ways in which Gramps helped him to be who he is – anywhere from his understanding of people, of himself, and especially of God.

Although Emmitt couldn't move or talk while in a coma, he did cry upon hearing of Spanky's and Gramps' death. The nurses became concerned when they saw his tears. Since they couldn't communicate with Emmitt, they didn't know what saddened him. All they knew was that something must really be bothering him.

"Do you think he heard us talking about his friend, Spanky, and his grandfather, Mr. O'Hara?" asked one nurse.

"Must be," replied another nurse. "Come on, you wipe the tears on the left side, and I'll wipe the tears on his right side."

In their compassion, the nurses did everything they could to let Emmitt know they cared.

Emmitt's Mom and Dad made the funeral and burial arrangements for Gramps in between their continuous trips back and forth to the hospital. A day didn't go by when they didn't visit Emmitt.

The coma was an airtight soundproof bubble where sound could be heard, but couldn't be let out. That's why Emmitt couldn't communicate with the outside world. And time moved differently in a coma. Hours moved like seconds and days passed like minutes. The week from Christmas to New Years passed like a flashing bolt of lightening.

On New Year's Eve, Emmitt was relaxing peacefully, lights off, his room as quiet as a cave. Suddenly, a deafening roar broke the silence. Dr. Clarence burst into Emmitt's room for his evening check-up checking his watch as he mumbled words to himself. "This is ridiculous! How can it be 7:30 already?" He stopped in his tracks when he noticed Nurse Matilda sitting silently in the dark room. "Maddy! You scared me half to death. What in the world are you doing here? Isn't it your night off?"

110

"Ain't no sign of any improvement and it's been a week since the accident," said Nurse Matilda, holding rosary beads in her hand. "Did yer hear about Ms. Annie's accident at the airport the night Master Emmitt got hurt in the snow?"

Dr. Clarence nodded.

"She passed out cold when she heard the news about Mr. O'Hara dyin' in his room. Then she heard about Master Emmitt – oh, it was just too much for that poor girl. Cracked her head wide open on a concrete floor in grief, she did." Ms. Maddy broke down and cried as she watched Doctor Clarence study Emmitt's medical chart, then his watch.

Dr. Clarence did the best he could not to look at Nurse Matilda. He didn't want to embarrass her further. "Yes, I heard all about her misfortune from her husband." The Nutty Professor looked out the window, shaking his head in distress. "We were able to stop the bleeding in her head with forty-two stitches. But I don't know how to treat her grief." The Nutty Professor closed Emmitt's medical chart with a sigh. He, too, shared in Ms. Maddy's grief.

"Doctor," murmured Nurse Matilda. "My Mama Francis once told this girl that there ain't no relief for grief. If you don't cure Master Emmitt, we're gonna lose Annie-girl to sorrow. And that's the truth."

"Maddy, you're putting undue pressure on me. That's unfair!" He turned to Nurse Matilda in irritation. "Don't you understand I can't treat a coma with medicine? It's a waiting game. I can't do anything further for Emmitt. His fate is in the hands of God." Doctor Clarence walked to the window and shook his head back and forth. "Maddy, why would a God of love and kindness allow this type of thing to happen to a nice innocent kid? It's doesn't make sense to my educated mind? What's missing?"

"Doctor Clarence, my Granny Mae told this girl somethin' on her death bed a long time ago that yer might need to hear."

Doctor Clarence raised his eyebrows and looked at Nurse Matilda with curiosity.

"Granny Mae woke me the day she was gonna die. I was sleeping in a chair next to her bed. Then she woke me with a snap of her frail fingers like they were young again. Suddenly, white splintering brightness began to shine from her eyes and lit up the dark room. *Young child*, she said, grabbing my hand. *I've been called! I saw the other side of time where rainbows are made and answers are given. Death is not the end but a new beginning.* Then the room darkened again and she passed on, just like that."

The Nutty Professor stood silently in thought, spellbound by the tale.

"Sometimes, I think I imagined the whole thing," continued Nurse Matilda. "But then again, I know in my heart it really happened. Life is hard to figure out sometimes, but I know that God is good and kind and there is a purpose for everyone and everything in this world."

"Maddy, thank you for sharing that story with me. I guess it comes down to accepting in faith that things are what they are for a reason beyond our human understanding." Dr. Clarence looked at Emmitt. Somehow, he had this feeling that Emmitt could hear their every word.

And indeed Emmitt could. He had listened to the whole conversation between the Nutty Professor and Nurse Matilda. He was as worried about his Mom as they were about him but he believed, without a doubt, that something good would come from this terrible accident.

Chapter 44
Private Talks

It was New Year's Eve at eleven forty-five at night and all Emmitt could do was lie on his bed. But he wasn't worried. He had this feeling that his coma was just a temporary stopover somewhere in time and space, a place where he could refuel and recharge himself for his next trip with Hans.

Although E.T.'s eyes were closed, he could visualize more now than ever before.

During the day, people occasionally came into the room to either read a book to him, pray over him or talk to him in private.

The conversation that stood out most was Billy's private talk with Emmitt. Billy spoke to Emmitt with tears in his eyes. The tears alone made Emmitt want to reach out and give his brother a mighty hug. But he couldn't. And this saddened Emmitt as much as seeing Billy cry.

113

"Emmitt, you have every right to hate me," said Billy. "But I promise to treat you better when you wake up." Billy paused to wipe away a tear. "Please wake up, Emmitt. I hate seeing you like this. It hurts so much. I'm sorry I was so rotten to you over the years. I promise when you wake up, I'll be the best brother a kid could have." Billy put his head on his brother's chest and wept. He could no longer hold back the flood of tears. When no more tears would come out, Billy continued. "J.C. Pepperweather needs you to come home and I need you to explain to Mom and Dad that I had nothing to do with your accident. I don't mind being grounded for the rest of my life but I do mind not having you around. Get better for me. Okay?"

Billy looked at Emmitt, hoping and praying that he would wake up. But Emmitt couldn't, as much as he tried. Billy kissed his brother on his cheek and left. If he had stayed for just another minute, he would have seen Emmitt's tears, tears that had Billy's name written on each drop. And each drop represented all of Emmitt's love for his brother.

Nurse Petersen's private talk was also very special to Emmitt. Finding Emmitt helpless and lost in the snow had opened her eyes to an important thing lacking in her life – compassion and sympathy.

"Emmitt, I want you to know that because of you I've finally realized why I've been so sad. I have nothing in my life. I have no one to love. But seeing you in the snow made me realize how fragile life really is. From now on, I'm going to do my best to love everyone. And I don't care if they don't love me back. I don't even care if they laugh at me. So, please wake up. Wake up so you can see how you've changed this old witch into a new person."

Emmitt couldn't believe what he was hearing. How could a little person, such as himself, change someone so drastically, he thought? But he was so moved by her words. He hated not being able to move or talk. Nurse Petersen deserved a big hug – an Emmitt-sized hug.

Part VII
The Master Plan

Chapter 45
Flying Upward into the Clouds

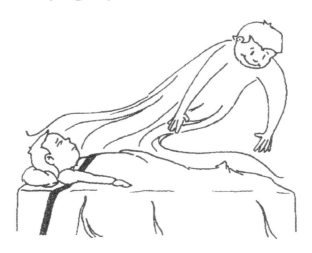

    Emmitt's parents left him alone in his hospital room at eleven fifty-five. They walked hand in hand to the hospital's cafeteria for a cup of coffee. It saddened Emmitt that they would have to celebrate the new year with coffee instead of champagne.

    At least there was the New Year's Eve celebration on the intensive care unit. But at eleven fifty-nine, the party had to be cancelled. A frightening alarm rattled from the machines monitoring Emmitt's heartbeat.

    To Emmitt, however, the alarm meant happiness. For it was time. Hans was back! And there he stood in the doorway, as chipper and giggly as ever.

    Emmitt knew what to do without being told. He lifted himself off his bed and left his body. He flew around the room with Hans on his tail. It was strange seeing his human body resting on the bed. It was like looking in a mirror. But Emmitt knew this was no mirror. This was the moment he had always waited for – freedom!

But not everyone shared Emmitt's elation. The room below erupted into a spasm of frenzied activity. Nurses and doctors rushed to Emmitt's bed. They pumped him full with drugs, injected needle after needle into him and zapped him with electric therapy. They did this to keep Emmitt alive. Little did they realize that Emmitt didn't want to be revived. He wanted to be forever free.

The chaos grew to a crescendo when the machines monitoring Emmitt's life support hummed a flat tune. And that, as many know, was the bugle of death. "Anaphylactic shock! Code red! Get Dr. Clarence! Hurry, before we lose him!" screamed a nurse.

Emmitt watched all this from above with alarm. He was happy that his Mom wasn't around, because the horrifying sounds in the room would have caused her to faint and hurt herself again. Couldn't these doctors realize that he didn't want to go back to his body? It was so much better to be able to fly.

Emmitt knew it was time to leave. The quickest way out was the window. And that's what he did. He followed Hans and flew out the window, flying upward into the clouds . . . to his one and only Star.

Chapter 46
The Tunnel of Life

    Emmitt and Hans flew through a tunnel of brilliant, glittering colors. They flew at the speed of light. Emmitt couldn't believe his eyes. It was too perfect and unimaginable. Yet, it was happening. He was flying with Hans Orion. And they were flying to heaven.
    Emmitt no longer needed his mouth to talk. He could communicate just like Hans did – with the mind. In fact, Emmitt no longer had to look. He could sense everything around him without looking at it.
    Just now, Emmitt sensed gentle music in the puff and pillow of the clouds, in the very breeze of the wind. He could finally hear the music of life as it was meant to be heard.

119

And he saw with his eyes and with his mind the things he always imagined. He saw snowmen bathing without melting; bunnies hunting for eggs and dancing to "bunny rock around the clock" songs; toothfairies smiling as they sang songs, showing off their beautiful new found teeth.

It was a wonderland of the imagination. And it was right before Emmitt's eyes. No longer did he have to imagine it. He could see it!

At last, Emmitt knew he was in paradise. At last, Emmitt knew that his faith in the Lord was not in vain.

Chapter 47
The Library

Emmitt lacked nothing.
Surrounded by green pastures and quiet waters,
He felt restored.
He belonged here.
And here he had David's strength and his courage.
He could fight a thousand giants without getting a scratch.

Hans and Emmitt stopped at a door that read:

THE LIBRARY
Knock and you shall <u>be</u> heard . . .

Emmitt knocked once. The door opened. To Emmitt's utter delight, the Master himself opened the door.

The Master's arms were stretched as wide as they were on the cross. So much light emanated from His aura that Emmitt could hardly look at Him. But he didn't need to look anymore. He could feel the Master as He embraced Emmitt with all the warmth and love of eternity.

If Emmitt thought he had reached paradise, then nothing prepared him for the bliss of the Master's hug. Everything else paled to that embrace, so encompassing it was.

No eye could see,
No ear could hear,
No mind could conceive,
What Emmitt felt at this moment.

He was embraced by the very dream of heaven.

Chapter 48
The Throne of Glory

"Welcome Emmitt, welcome Brother Hans," greeted the Master. The Master motioned with his hands, which were still scarred by nail marks, for Hans and Emmitt to sit down at the foot of His Throne of Glory. They both rested their heads on his legs. The Master caressed their heads with His gentle but powerful touch.

Behind the Master's throne was a window through which Emmitt could see the gate to Paradise, much the same way the hospital window had overlooked the rolling hills of the hospital landscape.

123

But this was no window in a hospital. This was a window in Heaven. And all things in Heaven are magical. The window slowly fogged into a silvery frost and transformed into a gigantic movie screen. And Emmitt got to see whatever he wanted. Even his own thoughts, right there on the screen. But something bothered Emmitt. He saw himself on the screen. He was lit up like a lightbulb. What did that mean? Something nagged at the back of Emmitt's mind. Could the light have something to do with his body on earth? Could his body still be alive?

Emmitt hoped he never had to see his disabled body again. He closed his eyes and prayed for this. When he opened his eyes, the screen was blank and to his pleasant surprise the window replaced it. What pleased him even more was what he saw through the window. The gate to paradise. This was the bliss Emmitt had always prayed for more than anything else. And it was there, just a hop, skip and jump away.

Chapter 49
Enter My Peace, Forever . . .

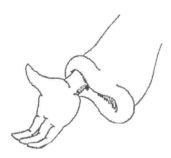

Emmitt heard a knock on the door. He turned around, and broke out his biggest smile when he saw Spanky and Gramps enter.

The Master spread his arms and welcomed Spanky and Gramps with his thoughts. "Paradise is yours."

Then the Master spoke with his hands raised high over his head. He waited a moment until the thunderous roar of approval from the people of his Kingdom subsided.

"FOR I WAS . . ."

HUNGRY . . . and you gave me food,
THIRSTY . . . and you quenched my thirst,
STRANGE . . . and you welcomed me,
SICK . . . and you cured me."

Spanky and Gramps were baffled. They asked simply, "When did we do this for you, Master?"

The Master pointed his finger at Emmitt. "I speak the truth. What you did for the least of my lonely and unwanted brothers and sisters, you did for me. Forever enter my peace!"

Gramps spoke with a spark in his eye as he walked towards the gate of Paradise with Spanky. "Imagine that. My own Emmitt cared for me the same time I cared for him. Who would have thought by serving him I served myself?"

Gramps hesitated a moment before walking through the gate of Paradise. He turned to Emmitt and spoke to him with his mind. "Thank you so much for helping us grow into children of God. Forever is more than a lifetime in these parts. To you we are eternally grateful."

"No need of thoughts," said Emmitt. "Your appreciation is evident in your love. Up here I am your brother. But I shall always know you as Gramps. And you shall always have my love. Now, go visit grandma. Your eternity lies through those gates up ahead."

Gramps hesitated. What could possibly be wrong? Then Gramps flew back to Emmitt and pleaded with him, not loudly but in a whisper. "Emmitt, my dear boy, please, you must go back. Your Mother will die without you. Bitterness and hatred will steer her off the course of love. Help her. Help her get here like you helped me."

Emmitt couldn't believe what his Gramps was asking. It was so unfair. But the thought of his mother weeping and crying, tormented and desolate, was more than Emmitt could bear. The very desire that wanted to make him leap through the Gate of Heaven also kept him still. He couldn't leave his mother. And the reason was love. It was as powerful as his desire to be in Heaven. In fact, it was one and the same. Emmitt knew he had to go back and save his mother. Having decided his course, he smiled.

Gramps knew what that smile meant. Emmitt would follow his heart. Fortified with this knowledge, he turned away and flew behind Spanky through the gates of Paradise. But not before throwing Emmitt a wink. All the children of Heaven cheered them along.

Chapter 50
He Came To Serve -
Not To Be Served

The Master spoke to Emmitt with a glorious smile on His face:

"It's time to make a choice!
What will it be, my little angel?
Relax in the comfort of my kingdom
Or
Return to your body?"

Emmitt looked at the holes in the Master's hands and feet, at the terrible marks still visible on His back and forehead. It was then that he knew he had made the right decision. His mother needed him more than ever.

"I'm going back, Master. I have to go back! Billy needs an alibi for the accident, Nurse Petersen needs more practice in the art of compassion, and my dad needs me to teach him Gramps' lessons of wisdom. But most of all, mom needs me. And I got to get to her before she steps off the path that'll lead her to here."

The Master grinned. He knew his child would make the right decision. And it wouldn't be long before he would see his child Emmitt again. In the mean time, He would content Himself with watching and guiding Emmitt while he grew on earth.

Emmitt had to follow His star . . .
To serve, not to be served . . .
To give, like His Master gave . . .
To shine like His Master's brilliance.
He needed to follow His Master's footsteps!

The birth of goodness . . .
The good news that everything was created in love . . .

"BORN UNDER A LUCKY STAR"

The End

EPILOGUE
The Riddle of the Stable:
Faith is the Answer

My story had to end, so your story might begin.

Did my story confuse you and make you sad?

Why did such bad things happen to the nice people in this story?

Do you believe that everyone and everything in this world is precisely arranged for a particular purpose? If so, you took the first giant step in explaining the following:

Why is a baby born, medically fragile, like E.T.?

Was it fair for a nice little girl like Spanky to suffer the pains of an incurable disease?

Why did Gramps have to die and leave his loving family on Christmas Eve?

These questions have been explored in this story and also in another book, the Holy Bible. Many stories of the Bible are also very difficult to understand when you use your mind alone. But the mind will only take you so far in matters of God and the Bible. To truly understand God, one must seek with one's heart, above all.

To Share Like He Shared,
To Serve Like He Served,
To Give Like He Gave,
To empty ourselves for the benefit of another . . .

When you understand the riddle of the stable, you will find a little bit of heaven on Earth!

Oh, by the way, J.C. Pepperweather was sent from above to cheer up E.T. You see, the Master doesn't forget anything in the circle of life, where everything and everyone has a vital purpose.

Be happy in the thought that **you** were especially created in love.
The End . . .

OR THE BEGINNING . . .
THE CHOICE IS YOURS.

Born Under A Lucky Star was written to help each and every one of us to accept, instead of question, who and what we are.

May the force be always with you . . .
In Peace . . .
Joy . . .
And Everlasting Happiness!

Also By Anthony L. Morrone
The Vanity Mirror...
a note left behind

ABOUT THE AUTHOR:

ANTHONY MORRONE is an accountant by trade, a little boy at heart, a storyteller by choice and the author of Born Under A Lucky Star.

Mantra - When life is hard to stand, simply kneel...because kneeling stands above all (in faith of mind). -Don't try to steer the river...RATHER let go to the flow of the universal power....accept it's daily adventure in total faith of mind, keeping stillness inside with a reflecting smile, outside.

Imagine the impossible into reality by simply energizing attention to our intention... Creating miracles (when you make a choice you can change the future).

To the reader: I once heard the expression that the best things in life cannot accurately be expressed in human language, while the things that can be expressed in language are easily misunderstood. This statement is not true for my editor and friend, PAUL UNDARI.

Paul is a lawyer by degree, an intellect in mind, a screenplay writer by choice and the editor of Born Under A Lucky Star by request. His fingerprints are smudged on each page of this book, thank you for the brilliant editing. Your patience is exceeded only by your skill.

COVER DESIGNED BY: FREYDOON RASSOULI

RASSOULI is an artist who reveals a mystifying artistic ability in his paintings. Through deep spiritual concentration he transcribes an image from his sub-conscience onto canvas. He calls his unique painting style "Fusionart" because it brings together Eastern and Western Cultures. Like an expanding universe, there is an ancient mystery about his work that can be experienced and discovered as the viewer reaches higher consciousness. Rassouli lives and paints in Southern California. His recent works can be viewed at: www.Rassouli.com

ANTHONY'S DAILY TO-DO-LIST

Be
- ~~buy~~ presents~~s~~

- wrap ~~gifts~~   Someone in a hug

- send ~~gifts~~   Peace

Donate
- ~~shop for~~ food

Be
- ~~see~~ the lights

Made in the USA
Monee, IL
27 June 2023

37774193R00083